THE CORNBREAD LETTERS

THE CORNBREAD LETTERS

T.E. LANE

IE Snaps
by
IngramElliott

Published by IngramElliott, Inc.
www.ingramelliott.com
9815-J Sam Furr Road, Suite 271, Huntersville NC 28078

Book formatting by Creative Publishing Book Design
Cover design by: H.O. Charles

ISBN Paperback: 978-1-952961-05-2
ISBN E-Book: 978-1-952961-06-9

Library of Congress Control Number: 2021938593

Subjects: Fiction—General. Fiction—Mystery and Detective General. Fiction—Thrillers / Supernatural.

Published in the United States of America. Printed in the United States of America.

First Edition: 2022, First International Edition: 2022

For Brandon, who filled my life with color.
And for Kim, who painted it.

Artwork by Kim Starkey Calvert

PROLOGUE

Sirens wail outside the building, and smoke fills the stairway. Conrad Bane Sr., a mountainous silver-haired firefighter, hoists a fallen rafter from the leg of his partner, Bill.

"Hang in there, Bill. We're gonna make it," Conrad shouts through the static of his radio. Damn thing hadn't worked right all day.

Bill's leg spills blood. Conrad picks him up like a baby. Bill eyes Conrad and says, "I didn't realize it would go this fast, Connie."

"Yeah, we just got a radio warning. The South Tower is down." Conrad wavers under Bill's weight in full gear.

Bill grabs Conrad's arm in a death grip and stutters, "No, man. Not the towers. I mean *our lives*."

Conrad stares at his friend as a bright white light illuminates their faces. Both men look toward the source of the light, frozen.

⁂

In a Brooklyn cemetery, Conrad Jr., a handsome copy of his dad, stands with his brother, Jeffrey. The young men hold their mother up, clutching her elbows. Streams of black mascara wash down Candy's face, foreshadowing the coming rain. She throws a single red rose on her husband's casket. Jagged lightning, punctuated by the crash of thunder, paints the scene bright white.

match flares. Michelle Bane lights two candles on a
fire truck-shaped birthday cake. Wilson claps as his
father, Jeffrey, fixes a plastic firefighter's hat on his son's head.
Michelle and Jeffrey sing an out-of-tune "Happy Birthday"
song to the boy.

Wilson blows out the candles as Jeffrey claps and pushes
a pair of thick tortoiseshell glasses up on his nose. Behind
them, Michelle pulls a large turkey from the oven. She blocks
the fridge door, which holds a recent family photo pinned to
the front.

In the picture, Wilson sits on the shoulders of his Uncle
Conrad. Next to them, his father, Jeffrey, has an arm around
the boy's grandmother, Candy. The adults display signs of
aging—Conrad Jr. has slightly graying hair, Jeffrey wears
glasses, and Candy is wheelchair-bound with an oxygen tank.
Wilson, only a few months younger than he is now, yanks
on his Uncle Conrad's New York Fire Department T-shirt,
choking him.

Standing over the high chair, Jeffrey tickles his son and sniffs the air. "Mmmm," he says. "I smell Turkey Day."

Michelle places the steaming turkey on the counter. "Lord, yes," she says with a twang. "And only a week late." She blows a curly brown bang out of her eyes with the corner of her mouth.

Jeffrey picks off a piece of crispy skin and pops it in his mouth.

Michelle smiles and grabs cranberry sauce, paper plates, and plasticware from a stack of moving boxes.

Jeffrey pats her behind. "I told you I'd get you back to North Carolina one day, Ms. Southern Belle."

"'Bout time, you big Yank," Michelle says. "I sure did miss me some sweet tea." She smiles and slurps from a giant yellow fast-food cup.

Jeffrey hands a piece of turkey to Wilson, who wriggles to get out of his chair. His dad deposits him on the floor.

"Let's eat all the turkey before Uncle Conrad comes ova'!" Jeffrey says.

The toddler points to the picture on the fridge. He chants, "Corn . . . na' . . ."

"That's right," his mother replies, eyeing the fridge photo. "That's your Uncle Conrad before he followed us down here from New York."

Wilson shakes his head no and points again. He chants, "Cor . . . ned, cor . . . ned, cor . . . ned!"

Jeffrey and Michelle follow their son's finger to a turkey-shaped platter on top of the fridge. Wilson bites the air.

"I think he wants some o' your Grandma Britt's cornbread," Jeffrey muses. "You know, from our visit to NC last year."

Michelle retrieves the platter and hugs it. "You're right. We served it on this platter. Thanksgivin' was the last time she baked her famous southern cornbread." Michelle studies the floor in reflection. Her brown eyes water.

A mail truck screeches outside. Michelle peeps through the kitchen window and mutters absently, "I looked all over for her recipe, but I think I lost it in the move."

"Really? Sorry, babe," Jeffrey says. "Maybe your mom has a copy?"

Outside, the mailman delivers the mail and drives off.

Michelle shakes her head. "No, I asked her after the funeral. She couldn't find anything."

Michelle is on the verge of tears. She heads toward the front door. "I'll grab the mail," she says and dabs her eyes.

Outside, Michelle squints in the sunshine as she approaches the mailbox. She removes the mail and flips through the envelopes.

Inside, Jeffrey pours a glass of tea and musses his spiky brown hair in the window reflection. Wilson sings to himself on the floor, playing with his fire truck. Jeffrey looks out the kitchen window and sees Michelle open a letter.

Wilson throws a plastic fireman at his dad and laughs hysterically. Jeffrey is still staring outside.

Across the lawn, he sees Michelle cover her mouth. Her shoulders shake. Before Jeffrey can react, a gust of wind plucks the letter from Michelle's hand, carries it across the yard, and slams it against the kitchen window.

Through the glass, Jeffrey reads the letter. The handwriting is cursive, small and deliberate.

Is this what you were looking for?

Plain Old Cornbread
1½ cups white corn meal
3 Tbsp. flour
1 tsp. salt
¼ cup sweet milk
¾ cup buttermilk
1 egg
3 Tbsp. melted shortening
Heat greased iron muffin pan or skillet in 400-degree oven. Pour mixture into hot pan and bake until thin-bladed knife or toothpick comes out clean.

Love,
Grandma Britt

The letter falls from its perch on the window, zips back toward Michelle on the lawn, and folds itself back into the envelope. The mailman takes the mail out of the box. The letter is pulled from the mail drop at the post office. The letter is unsealed at a desk. The tip of a pen erases the writing from the stationery. A man holds the pen.

Sam Abernethy sits at the desk in his study. His nervous demeanor does not match his relaxed handsomeness, which is instead reminiscent of a dreamy professor dressed in uncomfortable suits despite preferring khakis. His crisp white collar and designer tie droop with sweat.

The heaving is the worst part, he thinks.

Sam's writing hand shakes in resistance to an unseen force. The pen, with a mind of its own, painfully scrawls out a recipe for cornbread.

For Christ's sake, I've never been to church. I don't even know if I believe in God . . . or heaven . . .

Sam stops writing, bends over, and ralphs in the small desk garbage can. It splashes on his expensive leather shoes. He wipes his mouth and stares at the letter.

. . . but I think I'm starting to believe in hell.

2

Three Months Earlier

The blackened shell of a large lake house smolders as the fire marshal and a few firefighters buzz around the site. Sam's hefty job-site boots crackle over burnt wood and soot.

Jack Beck, a ruddy forty-year-old with a good start on a Santa belly, hands Sam a charred wooden picture frame and wipes his ashy hands on obnoxious pink-and-green golf pants.

"Where are your coveralls?" Sam asks. He brushes a floppy brown bang from his forehead with his wrist.

Jack's Brooklyn accent has been tempered by years in the South. "The truck's in the shop. Forgot to grab my work bag."

Sam nods, pulls an extra pair of latex gloves from the pocket of his baggy coveralls, and hands them to Jack. "What's the story?"

"Two days ago, Mr. Reyes was tryin' to jump-start his Porsche with a spare battery. It sparked, and up went the garage." Jack snorts. "Dumbass."

Across the driveway, Mr. Reyes, an exceptionally thin older man, picks up a burnt fender, the last remnants of a sleek sports car. Sam brushes soot from the picture frame with a latex glove. The frame is empty.

"This guy clean?" Sam asks.

"Don't know. The fire marshal's office didn't find any obvious accelerants so far," Jack replies. "But the fire started in the garage, which is full of them."

"Gas cans, lighter fluid, oil . . ." Sam walks farther into the rubble. "All you need is a spark. The battery?"

"Found it melted into mush on the garage floor, where Reyes says he was changing it out," Jack says.

"Only one? What about the new battery?"

Jack shrugs. "They only found one melted blob."

He and Jack step into what used to be a closet. Jack pulls out the charred remains of a few items of clothing still hanging by a thread on the blackened closet bar. He holds up a dated flannel shirt and sizes up Mr. Reyes, standing near what used to be his three-car garage. The shirt is clearly many sizes too big.

"What do you think? Keto diet? Paleo? Vegan? All three?" Jack chuckles.

Sam inspects the shirt's tag, which remarkably remains intact. *Size 3X.*

Across the driveway, a silver Mercedes screeches to a stop and nearly hits the fire marshal. The very buoyant and very blonde Mrs. Reyes flies out of the car and yells at Mr. Reyes, arms flailing.

Jack hangs the oversized burnt shirt back on the blackened closet bar. It collapses.

"Concerned?" asks Sam.

Jack nods. "As a double-stuffed pepperoni pizza with my name on it."

Jack and Sam play pool in a musty corner of a dark and woody Irish pub. Jack puffs on a stogie.

"Turns out Reyes was into his bookie for over two hundred grand and mortgaged the lake house without Bitsy's knowledge." He exhales. "She was about to divorce him. So, Reyes thought he'd collect a little dough and pay off the knee-breakers first."

Sam easily sinks a ball into the corner pocket. "What'd he use? If he sparked the battery, it may not have been enough to slow burn and light up the gas or kerosene or whatever was nearby."

Jack holds up a bag of potato chips. A red-headed waitress slops two beers on the high-top table and eyes the large, unopened bag.

"After-school snack?" she quips.

Jack presents the bag to her and answers, "Evidence."

Sam raises an eyebrow.

"Well, the real thing's at the police station and barely recognizable, but I picked up a copy for our investigation."

"You guys cops?" the waitress asks.

Jack kisses her hand like Pepé le Pew. "S-I-U, madame . . ."

"What's that? The Serious Idiot Union?" She chuckles at her own joke.

Sam reads her name tag. "Actually, Brittany," he says smoothly, "SIU is the special investigative unit of the Adelaar Insurance Corporation."

Brittany smiles in spite of herself. Although heading toward forty, Sam's youthful face, choppy brown hair, and athletic physique still get him flirts from young women at bars.

Jack presents the potato chips like a game show hostess. "You see, Brittany, the fat in the potato chips acts like a natural accelerant for fire," he says. "Unlike gas or kerosene, however, it's untraceable. And a family-size bag like this, placed near the engine, with enough air—"

"Where was it?" Sam asks.

"Glove compartment," Jack replies. "Lit it up, threw it in the glove box, convertible top down, hood up and—"

"Boom goes the garage," Sam says.

Jack jerks a thumb at Sam. "This guy is so good. All he had to do was look at an empty picture frame."

The waitress shrugs, confused.

Sam interjects, "Some people take favorite photos and clothes out of the house before they burn it down."

The waitress sticks her pen behind her ear. "Well, I'll keep that in mind if I ever decide to torch this dump."

Jack takes a long drag on his cigar. "Some people are drawn to the flame. Maybe you're one of them, sweetheart."

Sam studies the nine ball and adds, "It's risky. Probability and risk. Determiners of success in business, life,"—Sam looks up at Brittany, then sinks the nine ball without taking his eyes off her—"and nine ball."

Jack grins and points a thumb at Sam. "Can you tell why they call him Serious Sam?"

A pretty blonde woman wearing a racing jumpsuit reads Jack's palms in pit row of a sparsely populated speedway.

"I definitely see activity in your professional life here, see?" Alex says. "And some fireworks in your love life too."

Jack claps a hand to his knee. "Who's the girl?"

"Kate," Alex says with a smile.

"My wife?" Jack mutters and throws up his hands. "I need to find a better psychic."

Alex laughs as Sam, wearing a matching *Stockcar Driving Experience* jumpsuit, joins them. Jack hands Sam a racing helmet, but Alex snatches it first and fastens it on her own head.

"You're not gonna let your little sister show you up again, are you, Abernethy?" Jack says with a smirk.

Sam shrugs. "Why monkey with tradition?"

Alex smiles at her brother. It's a smile he's seen before, and it reminds him of a Cheshire cat waiting to pounce. He can't help but notice his "baby" sister—now in her mid-thirties—still garners attention from some pit crew members walking by.

Alex lays a slender hand on Jack's bulky, hairy arm. "Jack, you know I always wear the pants in this family."

"Yeah, skydiving pants, motocross pants, snowboarding pants . . ."

Alex shakes the jumpsuit sleeve to allow a silver charm bracelet to snake toward her wrist. Her sun-kissed face is lined around the eyes and mouth a bit, but a curious, youthful energy dominates her presence. "Besides, I need a new charm for my bracelet," she says and holds up the bracelet for both men to see.

Sam inspects the silver charms hanging from his sister's wrist—a miniature mountain bike and a kayak jingle next to a tiny water ski and a parachute.

Sam sighs. "You take too many chances, Alex."

"Relax, Sammy. I'm covering the race for the paper. I thought it'd be fun to take a ride in the fast lane. Get the firsthand experience of what it feels like to go that fast."

Jack opens his mouth to make the obvious joke, but Sam slaps a hand over his partner's mouth. "Where's Hannah?" Sam says over the roar of three stock cars coming to a stop nearby.

Alex smiles. "Sorry, brother. You got trumped. She's out with Travis."

Jack swings an imaginary golf club and peers into the distance. "Uh-oh," he says, raising a hand to block the sun. "Boyfriend, one . . . crusty old Uncle Sam, zero."

Sam chuckles. "I know. I used to take her to see dinosaurs. Now I am one."

A heavy race car growls to a stop in the pit lane. The driver waves them in.

"Okay, I'm up!" Alex says, pulling on her helmet. "Thank your clients for me, Sammy."

"Wait—" Sam says.

It's too late. Alex wiggles into the passenger side of the number three's roll cage. A track attendant straps her in, and she waves at the men, beaming.

With a roar, the car carrying Sam's baby sister jets out of pit row in seconds. It takes the first turn flawlessly and disappears out of sight.

"**H**ey there, lovelies," Sam says to Alex, who sits next to birthday girl Hannah. Hannah smiles sweetly, which doesn't quite fit with the purple-tinted tips of her dyed-silver hair and tiny silver nose ring. Obviously inspired by her mom and uncle, who were both products of the neon decade, she looks like a throwback to new-wave junkies from the eighties.

Sam sits in a wicker chair opposite Alex and Hannah and orders an iced tea from a passing waitress. Sam hands a sparkly gift bag bearing a unicorn and rainbow to his teenage niece. Hannah smiles and uses her hands and arms in a quick series of sign-language movements: "Give me a break—I'm turning fifteen . . . not five."

Sam smiles. "But you'll always be five in my heart." He looks directly at his niece so she can more easily read his lips. Although she has partial hearing with the aid of in-ear devices, Sam pokes his chest twice, middle finger bent to sign "heart."

"Open it, silly bug," Alex says to her daughter with an exaggerated wiggly face, her brown eyes a golden hue in the afternoon sun.

Behind Hannah and Alex, cars and pedestrians roll by the patio of the café, which serves only a handful of tables. The after-work crowd heads purposefully toward garages and bus stops, anxious to begin their weekends.

"Guess what?" Alex says, grabbing a French fry and stuffing it into her mouth. "My editor says she loved my human-interest piece on the female stock car driver." She pushes a lock of dirty blonde hair behind a triple-pierced ear. "Thanks for that, by the way."

Sam nods and smiles as Hannah pulls a gift card to Art-Way from the unicorn bag and squeals with delight. "You can buy a lot of paint with that," Sam says.

Hannah jumps from her seat and hugs Sam unexpectedly. "Thanks, Uncle Sam. This is so great. But I'm into oil pastels now." Hannah speaks, but with a slight rounding of her vowels and muted consonants.

Sam looks at his sister over Hannah's shoulder. For a split second, his heart swells at the joy of the moment. It's been a long while since his teenage niece gave him a hug.

Alex seems to understand his thoughts without words, and her eyes water just a little.

"She's considering me for more editorial work going forward. Which is what I've been waiting for." Alex raises a hand for the waiter and writes with an invisible pen in the air, the universal sign language for *check please.*

"Now, for your Pulitzer . . ."

"Don't joke, Sammy. I will finally have a chance to write about something important that can make a difference in the world," says Alex.

"I'm not joking, sis," Sam says and grabs the check from the waiter before Alex can get it. "And for the love of Christmas, quit calling me Sammy."

Alex nods her head in agreement, then says, "Sure thing, Sammy."

Sam smiles.

Hannah signs, "Thanks so much!" to her uncle and stuffs her art-supply gift card and unicorn gift bag into a backpack covered with pins, badges, and iron-on patches, mostly of vintage new-wave bands from the eighties.

Sam stands to depart. "Happy birthday, Hannah Banana." Hannah grins at her uncle. He turns to Alex. "Gotta run and finish up some work before I head out."

Alex nods. "You're coming tonight, right?" Alex nods toward her daughter. "The art show?"

"Of course," Sam says. "Wouldn't miss it." Sam signs something to Hannah, and she signs back, laughing. Sam exits through the patio gate onto the busy street.

"What'd he say?" Alex asks her daughter.

Hannah throws her backpack over one shoulder. "Inside joke."

Alex smiles at what would have invariably been some reference to an eighties teen comedy film—one far too mature and raunchy for her young daughter. Alex recalls how much those babysitting nights meant to both of them. She opens her mouth to remind Hannah of the many nights she'd come home to Sam holding her in his arms, refusing to move even an inch for fear of waking her, but Hannah is already headed toward the door.

☙❧

"Your feast, madame," Sam says to Hannah, who sits in Sam's living room, feet up on the sofa.

Hannah grabs the pizza box and sets it on top of the sleek-lined midcentury wood coffee table in the center of the cozy room. Sam grabs sodas from the fridge in the connecting open-concept kitchen, and Alex pours herself a glass of wine at a granite island.

"Hannah, your work was so brilliant tonight," she says, signing at the same time. She takes a swig of the pinot noir.

Hannah gives her mom a thumbs-up and cracks open a soda. She says, "I liked Travis's watercolor."

Alex and Sam exchange a glance and smile. Her classmate, Travis, it seems, is all Hannah can think about these days.

Sam grabs a stack of paper plates and napkins and plops down in an overstuffed leather armchair across from Hannah. The dining table, an expensive modern set, sits unused and covered with work papers and files.

A low-hanging light casts a moody shadow over the dining room at the front of the house. Sam had loved the fixer-upper as soon as he'd set foot in it. Although he had contractors do most of the updates, he had put down new tile in the hall bath himself—a black-and-white pattern that he thought matched the midcentury bungalow look he was going for.

Hannah plops a huge, floppy piece of greasy, wonderful cheese pizza on doubled paper plates and noshes greedily.

Alex sits in another chair opposite Sam, and the little family eats together in silence for a while. "I'm nervous," Alex says.

Sam wipes his mouth with a paper towel. "You'll be great."

"I hope so," Alex says and gulps more wine. "I've been waiting for a story with some teeth."

Hannah pulls a tablet from her backpack and sketches on a drawing program.

"What are you covering?" Sam asks, not bothering to sign since Hannah is occupied.

"Either a planned protest downtown or a press conference the mayor is holding. Not sure which one yet." Alex gets up for a refill.

"Preference?"

Alex calls back over her shoulder, "Not really. The mayor is commenting on the teacher-pay initiative. The protest is probably my best bet for more action. . . . Did you know that the chemical company headquartered downtown has possible ties to terrorist financing?"

Sam nods. "Sounds vaguely familiar."

Alex checks her watch. "Oh, we better scram. Early morning tomorrow, either way."

After a quick cleanup, Sam walks Alex and Hannah to the door. Hannah hugs her uncle. Alex piles on in a three-way embrace.

As they walk down the driveway, Sam waves from the open front door. "Love you guys," he calls.

Alex yells back, "Ditto, big brother."

Hannah holds up a hand in goodbye.

As is always the case, Sam's heart breaks a little as he watches them drive away into the night.

Sirens wail as news vans race to a smoldering three-story office building. Smoke billows around the building's inconspicuous signage, written in both English and Arabic: AHZARTEC CORPORATE CENTER. Firefighters douse the final tentacles of flame waving from the roof of the charmless square building with a massive spray of water. Clusters of sooty demonstrators cough on the grassy lawn amid discarded posters. Emergency personnel attend to the injured and continue to hose down the blackened building. A reporter broadcasts a live feed of the destruction.

"Behind me are the remains of the US headquarters of Ahzartec," the white-toothed man says into his oversized microphone. "The formally US-owned global petrochemicals company was purchased last year by Saudi financier Ratib Saqr, who has alleged ties to terrorist financing in the Middle East." The reporter waves his hand to indicate the chaos behind him. "As you can see behind me, anti-terrorism protesters, using the event as another platform for their message, were caught

19

in the middle of what's being called 'a despicable act of arson' by the county fire marshal's office."

On the lawn near the broadcast, Jack approaches Sam, who chews aggressively on his lower lip.

"Fire marshal's calling it first-degree felony arson," Jack says, gnawing on a ragged toothpick. "Three people in the lobby died. Fifteen injured."

"Any suspects?" Sam says, rubbing his temples rhythmically.

"Not yet, but Connie says the back doors were propped open, and the gas lines were tampered with."

Sam wrinkles his brow. "Did they find any devices?"

"No, but witnesses saw flashes in the ceiling. They think a timer was used to ignite the first floor during the protest."

Sam purses his lips in contemplation. "Cell phone?"

"Didn't find one," Jack replies. "Do you really think this is Ahzartec? Do you think they sabotaged their own headquarters?"

Jack picks up a half-burnt sign that reads, "Catch the REAL terrorists: the US government."

Sam shakes his head. "I don't think so. They're not overinsured—their policies haven't changed for two years. I called the office and told them we'd look into it to make sure Ahzartec isn't in any way part of this"—Sam motions to the chaotic and disturbing scene—"mess."

Jack surveys the wounded demonstrators across the grass. "Someone wanted to make a point here. Let's just hope it's not our client."

Sam's eyes dart among emergency personnel and reporters. "I'm surprised Alex wasn't here covering the demonstration," he notes. "She's been dying to get on the political desk."

Jack discards the anti-war poster as a gurney carrying a covered body knocks him down.

"Jesus!" Jack shouts, rolling onto the grass.

As Sam bends to help Jack to his feet, he freezes. He stares at the passing gurney. A woman's hand dangles from beneath the sheet, exposed. The badly charred hand wears Alex's silver charm bracelet.

Sam blinks slowly in disbelief as a beam of sunlight hits his sister's shiny new race car charm. The brightness envelops the gurney, the lawn, the protesters, and the corporate center until everything turns white.

☙❧

Bright white headlights melt in the rain. A train of cars snakes through a gray cemetery. A large bird of prey soars overhead, cutting through the mist. Graveside, Hannah stands with Jack under a green tent. A minister speaks as an interpreter signs to Hannah, whose stony face is not in keeping with her purple-streaked hair.

Sam stands without an umbrella outside the tent several yards away. He is soaking wet.

The minister, in low and weighty tones, eulogizes. "Alex Abernethy was a fearless and passionate mother, sister, and friend. She passed while fulfilling her life's passion as a journalist. . . ."

In the tent, Hannah closes her eyes. She can no longer understand the minister's words.

In a nearby tree, Alex's spirit—a kaleidoscope of past, present, and future bodies—swings on a wooden plank conjured from memory. Untouched by the rain and unseen by the living, she watches her funeral with pleasant curiosity. With each arc of the swing, she transforms from the casually pretty woman of her recent life to the flawless-faced, blue-skirted schoolgirl of her elementary school days to the punk-rock, coal-eyed, spiky-haired teen she'd once been—just for fun.

"Alex was a generous soul, bringing light and energy to everyone she encountered . . ." the minister continues.

Alex nods in agreement and watches as mourners drop red roses onto the silver coffin.

After most of the bystanders depart, Hannah lies on the green-turf ground cover and pulls her raincoat over her like a baby blanket. At this, Alex's spirit snaps back to her most recent incarnation—Hannah's mother. She goes to her daughter, but her presence carries no weight, and her embrace remains unfelt.

Jack gently picks up Hannah and carries her toward the car. Jack's wife, Kate, sobs into a handkerchief and follows her husband.

Sam enters the empty tent and stares at his sister's flower-laden coffin. After a moment, Sam places a small silver angel charm on top. As he looks up, he catches the eye of Sara Parker, a thirty-something beauty. Sam and Sara share a moment of connection before Sam looks away. *How long had it been since he'd seen her? Alex's birthday two years ago? Maybe.* He appreciates her presence, but contemplating their shared history will have to wait for another time.

Back on the nearby tree swing, Alex's schoolgirl self swings higher and higher, clutching the ropes. As it had done before, and would do forever, the wooden seat snaps in half. Alex squeals and dangles upside down, holding herself up by the ropes.

Alex

Imagine being on a six-hour flight at thirty thousand feet. Say three hours into the flight you've already endured the kid in front of you bouncing, twitching, moving, and jerking his seat back for, oh, two of the three hours. (The still hour was only because he was asleep.) You know he's a kid and it isn't his fault and you'll have to endure the motion for another effing three hours.

That's what it's like for me here with all these people. They are bumping, jerking, and annoying the hell out of me, and I cannot escape them.

Some of them want me to tell them what's going on at home. Some of them want me to send messages to people I've never met. I have no idea why they think I can, and all I really want is some freaking peace and stillness.

Isn't that the promise of death, after all?

Hannah unpacks a bag in Sam's spare room. She places a laptop, a set of paints, and a photo of her mother and herself on the wicker dresser. The picture shows a young Alex holding Hannah as a toddler. Both mother and daughter hold batons of cotton candy in front of a carousel.

Hannah cries silently. She falls onto the bed, pulls a quilt over her head, and thinks about her mother. She loved—*loves*—her mother more than anything in the world. But sometimes it was hard being Alex's daughter. Alex had a light that attracted the world to her, but also a darkness that caused her to be risky and careless. Sometimes her emotions were too high, and always, always, in her silent world, Hannah felt them.

It was a strange connection. If her mother was down or upset, Hannah felt it in her bones and in her head. Sometimes Alex's dark moods gave her headaches, and Hannah was grateful for the silence at the end of the day when she was able to remove her hearing aids and just be quiet.

Having an infection as a toddler had permanently altered her perception of sound and curbed her ability to speak and understand speech fully. But she was able to make out general words and phrases with her hearing aid. Alex learned sign language so they could communicate quickly, and they both loved playing around with new signs and learning how to create a language all their own. There was no one more fun than her mom. And no one more passionate.

Here in her new bedroom, Hannah feels her mother's loss like a heavy weight on her shoulders and chest. She feels like she can't breathe. So instead, she sleeps.

❧

Later that evening, Hannah sits in her room while her uncle works in his home office. She perches on a stool pulled from the small white desk in the corner and stares at a blank canvas on an easel. She contemplates it for a minute, then dips a paint brush into a jar of red paint.

Sam walks past the open door and smiles at his niece. Hannah raises eyebrows, but her mouth won't form a full smile. When Sam mercifully trudges down the hallway, Hannah returns to the easel.

A bright red brush colors the white canvas.

An Adelaar Insurance sign looms high on a Charlotte sky-scraper. On the nineteenth floor, Jack hovers around the company lawyer, Ted. Sam sits listlessly behind his desk, surveying pictures of the burnt Ahzartec Corporate Center scattered in front of him.

Jack slams the desk with a fist and yells, "This is horseshit! We're the best arson team in this piece-a-shit company."

Ted nods and holds up a hand to calm him. A well-cut suit says "corporate attorney," but a college-patterned tie belies his North Carolina hometown roots. "I called Maggie and tried to convince her to leave you guys on the investigation, but she doesn't agree. Not much risk here. The client's coverage seems pretty standard, and Ahzartec hasn't filed an overabundance of claims in recent years."

"We'll just work the case anyway. Right, Sam?" Jack says, puffing out his chest. "We owe it to Alex."

Sam shrugs apathetically. His face is stony and dull.

Ted checks his watch. "Look, I have to be in court in ten." Ted pats Sam on the shoulder. "If there's anything you need, Sam . . ."

Ted mouths to Jack, "He gonna be okay?"

Jack shrugs and walks Ted out of Sam's office.

"Let me know if there's anything else I can do for him, Jack," Ted says, once in the hallway.

"Thanks, Ted," Jack says, closing the office door behind him. "Good luck today. Plaintiff or defense?"

"Defense," Ted says. "We're being sued for that industrial accident with the bus and the bike. The vic's wife will be on the stand today."

Jack cringes. "That's a tough one. You gotta do what you gotta do, my friend."

Ted nods and makes his way down the hall.

Back inside the office, Jack plops down in the chair opposite Sam. "That is some bullshit."

Sam nods vaguely in agreement. Behind the desk, he shuffles through files and comes across a small lumpy envelope. He shoots Jack a quizzical look and opens it. A charred silver eagle charm falls onto the desk.

Sam raises his head. "What's this?"

Jack leans over the desk. "Not sure. I found it at Ahzartec the day we—"

"Where was it?" Sam cuts him off.

"Near the entrance. Everything was such a mess there, nobody noticed it."

Sam inspects the tiny silver bird and stuffs it into his pocket.

10

On a stone wall bearing the school name Charlotte School for the Deaf, Hannah cozies up to Travis, a lanky blond teen wearing edgy black clothes. They sign to each other, flirting. A black SUV pulls up next to them. Hannah signs goodbye and gets in the car with Sam.

Sam turns to Hannah, nudges her, and says, "How was school?"

Hannah reads his lips and faces the window before muttering with a slight muffling of consonant sounds, "Boring."

That night, Sam and Hannah share popcorn on the couch. Closed captions appear on the television over an eighties action film. Both long for comfort, but neither speaks.

Sam spies a framed photo on the end table—a black-and-white beach photo of a young Sam, about seven, dumping sand on a four-year-old Alex. Alex's laughter echoes in his mind as Sam cracks a tiny smile. His moment of reflection is broken as he notices Hannah staring at him.

Later, Sam watches from the hall as Hannah paints in her adopted room. Sam enters and, upon getting her attention with a wave, opens his arms to hug her. Sensing awkwardness, he pats her on the shoulder instead and surveys her work. On the canvas in front of them, a blood-red bald eagle stares back at him.

☙❧

Sam and Alex, fully grown, scrunch in tiny chairs at a child-size play table. Sam scribbles in a reading workbook as Alex checks the tiny cake in her play oven.

"I don't wanna play school," mumbles Alex.

Sam taps the pencil on his lips like he's seen his teacher do. "One more test," he says, "then you can go." He shoves the workbook in front of his sister.

Alex sighs heavily, shuts the oven door, and colors on the test with a red crayon.

Sam is mortified. "That's not the way you do it! That's scribble scrabble, stupid head!"

Alex laughs and raises a toe toward Sam. "Smell my feet."

"No."

Alex pulls her socks off and smells her own feet. "They smell like chocolate cake," she says, smiling.

Sam ponders this.

☙❧

Sam bolts from his dream, sweating. The alarm buzzes. Sam shuts it off and falls back on his pillow. Turning onto his side, Sam's arm falls through Alex, who is perched on the bed beside him.

Alex watches her brother sleep. She morphs into her teenage self, complete with a spiky buzz cut and dark lips. She sticks out her pierced tongue and tries to poke Sam with a long black fingernail. He grunts in his sleep and turns over, waving at an unseen nuisance. Satisfied, Alex smiles and bobs her head to new-wave music heard only in her head.

11

Alex

Being here is like standing in line at the grocery store. You know you have a lot of good stuff in your basket, but really, you just want to get home and put your feet up. I honestly can't figure out what I'm doing here at all. Everything was going really well for me and Hannah at home. And believe me, that was no small feat. I was a screw-up most of my life. Sam kept me sane and helped me get Hannah out of a bad situation I had gotten us into. (Think loser husband and dead-end waitressing job.) Sam pushed me to finish school and get my degree, which I did. Hannah was little, so she doesn't remember much, but her uncle helped me raise her. He was there for us. And we were all so happy.

I was about to get my real sea legs at the newspaper with that Ahzartec story—I had two of the demonstrators on tape. They would have made the cut too, but . . . I remember talking to my camera guy, Chris, about cutting them into my report, but then everything goes really hazy. Like, stops.

And here I am. Those demonstrators were really close to me, and I wonder why I don't see them here. But then again,

I don't see anyone I know. Aren't I supposed to be met by, like, my parents? Or Gram, at least? Oh, crap. I gotta go—this nut job keeps trying to talk to me, and I want nothing to do with him. He's a huge bastard, like a silver-haired mountain.

12

Sam parks on a shabby neighborhood street and exits his black SUV. The old bungalow has seen better days. Partly obscured by tall grass, a burnt-out sports car with the rims and tires missing perches on concrete blocks. As Sam inspects the car and makes some notes, the bungalow's peeling white front door opens.

A little girl, disguised by grimy clothes and greasy blonde hair, skips out of the house holding a tattered military doll. The doll is naked except for a hula skirt and plastic high heels that have been wedged onto his flat feet.

Sam waves at her. "Hi there. I'm Sam."

The kid hugs the doll. She is shy but not afraid.

"Is your daddy home?"

She replies, "No."

The girl holds up her cross-dressed soldier. Sam smiles and scribbles in his notebook. "What's your name?"

"Abbie."

"Well, Abbie, your daddy called us because his car was vandalized, and the tires were stolen. I'm here to drop off a check for him."

Abbie gnaws on the doll's hand, which is already deformed from prior biting. She looks up at Sam shyly. "Do you want the tires back?"

℃℧

Inside the shabby house, Sam and Abbie overlook four tires and rims that fill a small bedroom. Sam cracks a wry smile.

In the living room, Abbie colors at the couch. Sam loosens his tie and says, "Can you tell your daddy to call me when he gets home?"

Sam wipes sweat from his brow and fans himself with his notepad.

Without looking up, she replies, "Our phone is broke."

"Well, maybe he can use a neighbor's phone?"

Abbie shrugs.

Sam looks at his hands. They are dripping with perspiration. Confused, he wipes them on his trousers as he waves goodbye to the girl and makes his way to the front door. Sam grabs for the tarnished door handle, which jumps out of the way. Sam stares at the door. A second later, the handle returns to its proper place.

He mutters to himself, "Long day."

Sam reaches again for the handle, which melts in his hand like hot caramel covering an apple. Dazed, Sam stumbles dizzily toward the couch. "What the—" Sam looks at the blurring girl and smiles weakly. He is ashy, green, and white all at once.

Abbie stops coloring and says, "You look funny, mister."

Before she can finish, vomit floods the coffee table. The girl screams and runs to the bathroom.

Sam moans, "I'm sorry. I'm sick." He falls onto the threadbare gold couch. His hand trembles violently. He attempts to steady it to no avail. Sam watches his hand, puppeted by an unseen force, grab one of Abbie's crayons. He drags the red crayon across the only remaining clean sheet of paper.

In the corner of the room, Alex's spirit gnaws a fingernail and watches Sam curiously.

13

Alex

So, I lose a lot of time here. Or time doesn't work like it did at home. I have dreams here about seeing Sam and Hannah, but I'm not totally sure I am asleep? It feels like I'm there with them—in spirit at least. Don't really know. I did find this area I call the construction zone. It's like at the edge of this place, and there are thick clear tarps hanging in a long row. They waver in the wind, and in some places I can kind of see through them, but it's hazy, like looking through a foggy windshield.

I can see the city and the house, and sometimes I can see Hannah painting. She's really getting good. There are times, also, when I am *called* through the tarps. It's hard to describe, but I think it's when Sam or Hannah is thinking about me at the same time I'm thinking about them. If I'm near the tarps when this happens, I am pulled beyond the tarps into their world. It doesn't seem like they can hear or see me, but sometimes I think they can feel me. It only lasts a few seconds, though.

And there is a downside. Big Gray has started bringing his friends to see me every time I visit the construction zone. Everyone thinks that I'm something special because I can see through the tarps. They don't even see the tarps. I don't tell them I go through sometimes—they'd never leave me alone.

Anyway, I'm worried about Sam a little. I think he's drinking too much, but who am I to talk? He sobered me up plenty of times when we were growing up pretty much on our own.

He's really been throwing back the whiskey since he saw Sara at my funeral. Interesting. I know things were strained when he and Sara broke up a while back, but she and I had started hanging out again, and I had hoped that maybe the three of us could put the past behind us. It had finally started to feel like I had my best friend back. And then . . .

Looking back, maybe I was too hard on both of them when they got together. They couldn't help that they fell for each other. I don't know . . . at the time, it felt like a betrayal. Like I was left out of the triangle we'd all created when we were kids. But now, seeing how hard this is on him, I wish Sam had someone. He could do worse than Sara Parker, that's for sure.

Anyway, water under the bridge, I guess. And speaking of bridges, where are my folks?

They've been dead for years. I was a junior in high school when the crash happened. A patch of black ice, a frozen bridge, and in an instant, they were gone.

Back then, after they died, I never dreamed about them, not even once. But I always thought that when I finally kicked the so-called bucket, I would get to see them again. Or feel their presence or whatever is supposed to happen when your family greets you at heaven's gate. I am not sure if this is heaven or not, though. Either way, what I wanna know is: where the hell are they?

# 14

Still in his suit, Sam gargles and spits into a blue glass sink. He remembers installing the fancy sink himself, spurred on by Sara when they were considering moving in together. She had loved the "infinity" spout—their own tiny waterfall.

Sam pulls his mind away from thoughts of Sara and their bound-to-fail love affair. He should have known getting involved with Alex's best friend was a mistake. He did, actually, know it was a mistake. He hadn't intended, though, for it to come between him and his sister. Or between Alex and Sara. They'd all been friends since high school—*the three drunketeers*—and had been inseparable until Sam started community college and Sara left for the state university, several hours away.

"Not now," Sam growls and forces himself to refocus on the more pressing issue. He pulls a piece of paper from his jacket pocket and sits on the closed toilet. He does not understand what happened to him today. One minute he was talking to the girl about the tires, and the next second he was—well, his hand was—scrawling out this letter using the girl's crayon. He shakily unfolds the paper to reveal the crude note he had . . . dictated? It's addressed to a Judge Francis Mason, a resident of Charlotte, even though he's never met or even heard of the guy. He cannot wrap his mind around the contents. It's very, very disturbing.

He stuffs the paper back into his pocket and joins Hannah for a pair of frozen dinners on the couch. As is her habit, Hannah heads to her room after the sitcom ends, and Sam sits alone on the couch with his thoughts. He spies the bottle of whiskey—a gift from Jack—unopened on the console near the window. *Why not?*

On his third glass, Sam reads the crayon letter for the fifth time, still uneasy. He downs the entire glass of whiskey in one gulp. After reading it one last time, he crumples the letter, walks to his home office, and tosses it into a small garbage can under his desk.

Unseen by Sam, Hannah watches her uncle from the dark hallway and creeps back into her room.

∽

After midnight, Hannah walks silently through the dark hallway. She checks to be sure her uncle's bedroom door is closed, and then sneaks into his study. She approaches the desk and removes the crumpled paper from the garbage can.

Judge Francis Mason
34405 W. Fahrenheit Way
Charlotte, NC 28269

Dear Daddy —
I don't know why you did what you did. I met a friend
here in the white place and she told me it wasn't my fault.

It doesn't hurt anymore. My friend don't know why you would have burned me, Daddy. She said I am real pretty.

Love,
Cecilia

Hannah bites her lip. Her eyes are flat white saucers, and she doesn't understand why her uncle has this letter. She looks out the study window at the full moon hanging high in a dark-blue sky. Across the cloudless white sphere, she sees the shadow of something. It has wings and soars across the moon in full flight. *The eagle.* She knows what she must do.

Hannah quietly rummages around Sam's desk until she finds what she's looking for—an envelope. She folds the crayon letter and addresses it to Judge Francis Mason. She seals the envelope, applies a stamp, and sticks it into her pocket.

Hannah returns to her room and pulls out her easel. She sets a blank white canvas upon it and strokes it, considering the nature of blank spaces. Hannah pulls out her caddy of paint, its bright colors sharing space with muted pale tones. After running her finger over the tin lids, she finally selects a jar of pale lavender. She pours a dollop of paint on her palette and dips a thin brush into the creamy acrylic. She places the brush on the canvas and begins. The curve of a hooked beak begins to take shape.

Hannah doesn't know where the birds come from. She's painted at least five of them so far—red, black, blue, green, and now lavender. Ever since she came to live with her uncle, it's all she can paint. She meant to search online, but she's pretty sure it's a bald eagle. She saw one once when her mom took her to the North Carolina Raptor Institute, the hospital for birds of prey. She tried to fight it once and paint a flower, then a house. Anything other than the bird. But nothing else comes. She feels better once it's out of her.

Hannah smiles and wraps up the beak detail. A few more strokes and done. She wipes purple paint on a smock and sighs. Thank God. Now she can sleep.

15

The doctor's office is cold, like any other. Sam examines Dr. Brenda, his longtime general practitioner, as she examines his MRI results. Sam is aware of his stomach peeking through his open shirt. He waits a moment longer before buttoning it up.

"Your physical examination looks fine, Sam," Brenda says and clicks a button on her computer. She scans the screen. "Your scan shows nothing out of the ordinary. The nausea you describe could be related to migraines or stress."

The doctor removes her glasses. "It's normal to have anxiety related to the death of a loved one, Sam. I can refer you to a neurologist or psychologist if you'd like."

"No, no. Just wanted to make sure everything was okay. Physically," Sam replies. A moment of silence passes. "I read about this thing," Sam says, wavering. "A condition."

Dr. Brenda tilts her head to one side.

"Alien hand syndrome." Sam bites his lower lip awkwardly.

Dr. Brenda nods. "I've heard of it, but it's pretty far out there, medically speaking. It's usually associated with stroke victims. I didn't hear you describe any symptoms related to stroke, though. Do you believe stroke to be a possibility?"

"I don't think so. But the case studies I read about . . . this syndrome . . . like someone's right hand involuntarily yanking out the shirt tucked in by the left, and so on. One hand grabbing objects out of the other. It's how I feel when I'm writing. Out of my control." Sam waits. "I know it's a stretch, but—"

"When you wrote the letter you mentioned. The child's letter?" Dr. Brenda says.

Sam nods.

"Has it happened again?"

"No, thank God." Sam fidgets on the exam table.

"Well, we can get some neurological tests run to be sure, but the condition you mention is extremely rare," Dr. Brenda says without reaction. "It usually results from damage to the frontal lobe. It's true these patients have described spontaneous movements. There is no real explanation for it. I think we would want to see more evidence of these uncontrolled movements before we subject you to further tests. Do you agree?"

Sam and Dr. Brenda sit in silence a moment.

Eventually, Sam nods. "Yes."

"I'm happy to refer you for more tests, Sam. But what I really recommend is time. Give yourself some time," Dr. Brenda says. "I can recommend a grief counseling group or individual counselor. I'd like you to consider it."

Sam sighs and nods again.

"If you decide you want more tests, come back, and we'll look into other options." Dr. Brenda walks Sam to the door.

Sam shakes her hand. "Sure thing, Doc."

16

Jack walks down the city sidewalk with Conrad Bane Jr., known to Conrad's friends as "Connie." Sam catches up and hands both men a sloppy chili dog. Conrad swallows his nearly whole, wiping a splatter of chili on the sleeve of his New York Fire Department T-shirt.

"No comparison to the old neighborhood dogs, huh, Jack?" Conrad mutters, swallowing.

Jack hits him on the back of the head. "Manners, dickhead."

Conrad smiles and pulls back his fist. "Why, I oughtta . . ."

"To da moon, Alice. To da moon." Jack chuckles.

Sam watches the two friends, an outsider. He dumps the paper hot-dog bag into a trash can as the trio reaches the downtown Charlotte station, where they house the ladder trucks separately from the fire engines.

Firefighters mill about the open garage. Sam, Jack, and Conrad turn to watch a pretty brunette click by in heels. Conrad snaps the suspenders on his firefighter pants and whistles.

"Did you know," Conrad says, elbowing Sam, "Jack once talked the prom queen into giving him head during a high school football game? Under the freaking bleachers?!"

Sam raises an eyebrow.

Jack coos dreamily, "Ah, yeah. Susan Deager."

Jack and Conrad smile deviously and say in unison, "Eager Deager."

A young Latino interrupts the group and hugs Jack. "Jack-ay, my man! Haven't seen you around the hood lately."

"Paulo! What's shakin'?" Jack says with a fist bump.

"Livin' the dream, man," Paulo says with a wave toward the fire station. "What's new with you?"

Jack nods to Sam. "My boss here's got me workin' day and night."

Sam smiles.

Paulo snaps into a gyrating spin and moonwalks backward on the sidewalk, grinning. "Ow!"

Conrad is humorless. "Save it for the party, Paulo."

Unfazed, Paulo points a thumb at Conrad. "Can you believe this guy's gonna be *un padre*? Little did I know when my cousin introduced me to her 'nice friend Conrad' that she'd end up barefoot and pregnant. *Épocas locas.*"

Sam and Jack exchange surprised looks. Conrad beams as Jack gives him a shoulder squeeze.

"What? No way, man!" Jack says with a smile.

"Yep. Ariel's six months along now. The baby shower's Saturday. I hope you both can make it," Conrad says.

A fire siren interrupts the revelry. Paulo hooks suspenders over his shoulders and runs toward the truck. "Duty calls, *amigos. Mañana!*"

Sam and Jack wave goodbye, but Conrad lingers.

"Aren't you goin'?" Jack says to Conrad.

"No. I got a debrief with the police department and the fire marshal today," Conrad replies. "They're breaking my balls on this Ahzartec arson investigation. I was first on the scene, up close and personal with the DOAs—"

Sam freezes; his smile drops.

"Oh, sorry, man. I didn't mean anything," Conrad says, eyeing the sidewalk.

It's silent for a tense moment.

"I better go," Conrad says and jogs off. "Bye, guys."

Jack surveys Sam. "He didn't mean anything, man."

Sam clamps his lips together. "Forget it."

17

The house is quiet and dim. Sam reads in a chair, one hand occupied by a glass of whiskey, the other by a book titled *Theories of Channeling and Mediumship: The Nature of Supernatural Messages.*

Paintings of bald eagles, in every color and size, fill the living room behind him—Hannah's handiwork. Sam yawns and plops his feet up on the coffee table next to a stack of psychology books and a bottle of sleeping pills. Unable to resist any longer, he closes his eyes.

Sam and Alex, fully grown, spar in too-small karate outfits. Sam punches Alex hard on the arm. Alex wails and collapses to the ground.

Sam runs to her. "Alex! I'm sorry! Are you all right?"

Alex opens her eyes, grins deviously at her brother, and punches him hard in the groin.

Sam doubles over in pain.

Sam jolts from the dream, a hand on his crotch. A hard knock on the door yanks Sam fully awake. Sam approaches the front door and inches it open. Suddenly, it's kicked open full force, knocking Sam to the floor. He lands hard on his elbows and swears.

An imposing bald man pants and hovers over Sam. He holds an envelope in his hands.

"What kind of sick fuck are you?!" the man screams.

Sam scrambles to his feet and grabs an umbrella by the door. He hoists it high like a club. "Calm down, mister! I don't want to hurt you, but I will. Calm down!"

The sweaty man staggers backward onto a bench by the door and holds his head.

"My daughter's body was never found, do you hear me?" He looks up. "You better hope you don't ever end up in my courtroom, you fucker!"

Sam is bewildered. "I don't know what you're talking about! Who the hell are you?"

The man explodes from the bench, shoves Sam to the floor, and throws the envelope onto his chest. Before Sam has a chance to react, the man storms outside.

He yells back over his shoulder. "Don't ever contact me again, or I'll have you arrested, asshole!"

Sam scrambles to his feet as the man starts a black luxury sedan and screeches away.

"Jesus Christ," Sam says, his heart rate spiking. He breathes and inspects the envelope.

It's preprinted with his name and address—from the personalized stationery that Sara gave him years ago. The front of the envelope is addressed to Judge Francis Mason on Fahrenheit Way. Sam pulls out the crumpled letter inside. It's a white piece of paper with a note written in red crayon.

Dear Daddy —

I don't know why you did what you did. I met a friend here in the white place and she told me it wasn't my fault.

It's his letter, the one written in the little girl's living room. But how? He was drunk that night, but he has no recollection of sending the letter. There's *no way* he would have done that.

Sam darts his eyes wildly around the foyer, focused on nothing. He jerks his head toward the hallway. Hannah's door is closed. Sam closes the front door and locks it. He leans against the front door for a moment, breathing heavily.

A few moments later, he lumbers down the dark hallway and stops at Hannah's closed bedroom door. He hesitates a moment with his hand on the door. He lets it go—for now—and retreats into his own dark bedroom.

18

losing the door to his office, Sam presses his mobile phone to his ear and starts down the hallway of Adelaar Insurance.

"I found Francis Mason," Jack says on the other end of the call.

Sam can hear horns honking. "Where are you?"

"Downtown. Lunch with Kate."

"What'd you find out?"

"Long career with the New York DA's office before becoming a judge. He moved to Charlotte last year after suing his former employer for character defamation." Jack's voice crackles on the line.

"Based on what?" Sam turns a corner and continues down a corridor dotted with corporate offices.

"Allegations linking him to a missing boy at his daughter's school. Grand jury didn't indict," Jack says, a car screeching in the background. "Shitballs! That was close."

"You okay?"

"Yeah, just a bus driver hell-bent on making his stop," Jack says with a snort.

Sam stops before an office door with a sign that reads employee services.

"Okay, thanks, Jack," Sam says into the phone. "Keep digging. I'm here—gotta go."

"Roger, dodger," Jack says. The line goes dead.

Sam hangs up and breathes deeply. He opens the door, resigned.

❧

Sam sits on a couch across from the company shrink, Dr. Sheila, who wears purple from head to toe.

"How many more sessions do we have?" Sam asks, squirming on Dr. Sheila's tweedy brown couch.

The purple shrink looks at Sam serenely. She waits a long, annoying minute before replying. "We've been over this, Mr. Abernethy. The company requires at least six sessions after a major personal tragedy. To help ensure you are able to return to work effectively."

Sam nods.

"But what's more important is that you feel you are ready to move on," she says, grabbing a tissue from the coffee table and dabbing at her nostrils. She clutches the tissue in her long fingers like a gun.

"I'm ready," Sam replies, mustering as much believability as he can. He smiles awkwardly.

The purple shrink nods and scribbles in a leather-bound notebook. "Are you sleeping?" she asks without looking up.

Sam considers this a moment. "Yes. But I have dreams."

Dr. Purple's head pops up like a velociraptor sensing prey. "Really? What kind of dreams? Of your sister?"

Sam nods. He instantly regrets this. He imagines the doctor pouring over dream-interpretation reference materials and itching to try her hand at deciphering his.

"Tell me about them," she says, eyeing Sam intently.

Sam's gaze is stuck on her hair. It's in a very puffy, twisted knot atop her head. He can't help but think it looks like a cinnamon bun and realizes he hasn't had a Cinnabon in a while. There's a location near Hannah's school. Maybe he'll take her for one later this afternoon.

"Sam?" Dr. Purple says, jogging him from his baked-goods stupor.

"Sorry."

"What were your dreams about?" The doctor blows her nose unceremoniously and stuffs the tissue into a pocket of her long lavender vest.

"I don't know. Childhood stuff." Sam looks at his shoes. Then at his watch.

"Am I keeping you from something?" Dr. Purple asks stiffly.

Sam shrugs. "Lotta case work."

"Is something else bothering you, Sam?"

Sam and the doctor lock eyes in an unspoken battle. Sam's face reflects the struggle—to tell or not to tell. His stomach churns. It's on the tip of his tongue. He wants to expunge every detail of the last few weeks—the dreams, the crayon letter, the visit from the judge . . .

Fortunately, logic wins. "I'm just frustrated with the case," he says, backing off. "There's no suspects—the police have nothing. I want to know who did this." Despite himself, Sam's face pinkens. He recognizes these feelings are real. He really *is* frustrated.

Dr. Purple sits back in her chair and removes her glasses. "I thought they took you off the Ahzartec case," she says, finally.

"They did."

The purple shrink raises an eyebrow in disapproval. She looks at her own watch. "Until next time, Mr. Abernethy."

Sam hops up from the couch a little too enthusiastically.

19

Sam and Jack approach a modest-sized canary-yellow house guarded by a statuette of the Virgin Mary and urns of plastic flowers. Sam carries a bottle of whiskey adorned by a blue bow. A line of vehicles and Latino music betray a party in the backyard of the house.

"Let's go around," Jack says, and makes his way around the side of the house.

On the back patio, the baby shower is in full swing with a band, baby-blue balloons, and a keg of beer. Party guests, including several firefighters in local fire department T-shirts, pat Conrad on the back and offer congratulations.

Near the kitchen door, Jack and Sam watch the scene, beers in hand.

"I really shouldn't be here, Jack. It's a conflict of interest," Sam says.

Jack swigs his pale ale. "Connie's a friend, Sam. Relax."

"He's also testifying in the Ahzartec case. He was first on the scene, as he made clear the other day." Sam's face reddens at the memory of Conrad Jr.'s mention of the DOAs—dead on arrivals.

"Technically, we're not on the case anymore, remember?" Jack says, eyebrows raised.

Sam shrugs and gulps his beer in defeat.

Across the patio, Conrad Jr. hoists a small boy onto his shoulders and says, "Up you go, Wilson." Wilson giggles. Wilson's mother, Michelle, snaps a photo. She takes a sip from a super-sized yellow fast-food cup filled with sweet iced tea. Her curly brown locks are pinned up into a twist and decorated with a blue barrette.

A wiggly Wilson almost falls backward but is righted by his uncle Conrad just in time.

Conrad's brother, Jeffrey, pushes up his tortoiseshell glasses and lays an arm around a pregnant Hispanic woman. Jeffrey and Conrad share the same wiry, strong frame. Their coloring is similar except for the gray streaks in Conrad's brown hair.

"Don't worry, Ariel," Jeffrey says. "I'm sure my bro will be more careful with *your* kid."

Jeffrey laughs and fends off a playful punch from Conrad.

Ariel smiles. "I hope so."

Conrad lowers Wilson and kisses Ariel on the nose. "Trust me, baby."

Michelle waves a hand at everyone. "Get together, y'all. Family selfie."

Michelle attaches her phone to a selfie stick and raises it in front of herself, Jeffrey, Wilson, Conrad, and Ariel. Her phone flashes bright white, and they're frozen in time.

Near the kitchen door, Jack raises his beer bottle. Sam follows suit.

"I'd like to make a toast to my old friend, Connie." Jack's voice projects across the patio. He waves a hand at the band, and the notes wind to a stop. "Connie and I have been pals a long time"—Conrad smiles and nods in agreement—"and it's true we been through lots o' shit. Some we started ourselves, of course."

The crowd laughs.

"But some things no one should have to go through," Jack continues. "I never thought I'd see the day that Connie would settle down, but here he is, ready to be a dad—"

The crowd whistles and cheers.

"And I just wanna say, may he be the kind of father his dad was to all of us back in the city. Raise your glass to Conrad Sr., the best goddamn firefighter in New York City."

The crowd murmurs a mix of "To Conrad!" and "*Salud!*" and "*Enhorabuena!*"

Conrad and Jeffrey hug each other and echo, "To Pop."

Behind the brothers, Candy Bane rolls forward in an electric wheelchair. She wears a FDNY T-shirt and an oxygen tank. Years of smoking have left her looking ten years older than her age of sixty-nine. Oddly, she sips from a dainty porcelain coffee cup.

Conrad and Jeffrey bend down to kiss their mother on each cheek. She raises a skinny, gnarled hand to quiet the crowd.

She breathes heavily through oxygen tubes in her nose. "Gawd bless my boys, Conrad and Jeffrey," Candy says, wheezing. "And their . . . saint of a father, Conrad Sr., may he rest in peace."

A flash from Michelle's camera captures mother Bane and her two sons toasting the sky.

As the party chatter resumes, Jack is about to approach Conrad but stops short when Candy motions for her sons. Jack and Sam watch from the patio as Conrad and Jeffrey pull up chairs next to her in the yard.

Wilson runs and jumps onto his father's lap. Jeffrey kisses the toddler on the top of the head. Candy pinches Wilson on the cheek. The boy's lip quivers.

"It's okay, Wilson," Jeffrey soothes his son. "You remember your grandma Bane . . . from our trip to New York City. Where we saw Uncle Connie."

The boy calms a little but regards her tentatively.

Candy twists her mouth into a grimace and breathes deeply through the tubes in her nose. "What's the matter, little Bane? It's just your old granny. I brung you a present. How about that?" Candy says and reaches into a saddlebag attached to her wheelchair. She indeed presents a wrapped gift stamped with tiny trucks and cars to her grandson.

Wilson's eyes light up, and Candy wins a smile from the boy. As Wilson tears off the paper, Sam sees Michelle—who is talking with Ariel behind the clan—look up sharply at her son's squeal.

"What's this?" Jeffrey says, a little tentatively as Wilson unwraps a square leather case with a silver latch and a handle. Jeffrey looks quizzically at his mother, but Candy just smiles and nods for the boy to open the case.

Michelle shrieks first. She's on her son like a swarm of hornets, ripping the case from his hands.

Candy looks up at her, confused, from her chair. "What's the matter? Can't I give my grandson a family heirloom?"

Michelle's eyes blaze. She starts to open her mouth, but Jeffrey catches her eye. As she looks around the party, it's clear all eyes are on her. The music has stopped, and everyone stares.

Candy doesn't wait for an answer. "Boys—you remember your father's service pistol from his time in the army. He would have wanted his sons to have it. But there's two of you, so I think better for Wilson to have it." She nods at the leather case in Michelle's hands, in which can be seen a weathered revolver in a foam encasement, along with a box of bullets.

"Thanks, Ma," Conrad says, quickly closing and commandeering the box from Michelle. "We'll take real good care of it."

Wilson begins to cry. His father bounces him on a knee. "It's okay buddy, we've got your toys in the car. We can get one, yeah?"

Jeffrey and Conrad exchange a look as Ariel guides Michelle, wide-eyed and speechless, toward the drink table. Under her breath, Michelle mumbles, "Crazy old battle-ax."

Ariel chuckles and hands Michelle a fresh glass of sangria while she pours herself a club soda. "To the family," she says with a smile. Michelle chugs her sangria.

Conrad beckons Paulo with a wave of his hand and points to Candy.

Paulo, wearing a baby-blue party hat, jogs up to Candy and goes to refill her coffee cup with tequila, but the bottle is empty.

"No problem, I've got another at my place next door. I'll be right back, Señora Bane." Paulo lays a hand of comfort on Mrs. Bane's shoulder. She promptly removes it.

Unfazed, Paulo jogs with the empty tequila bottle toward the side-yard fence. He jumps it easily and disappears into his yard.

Conrad, gun case under his arm, passes Sam and Jack on his way into the house.

"What the hell?" Jack says.

Conrad just shakes his head and disappears inside. "Don't ask."

☙❧

Late that night, as the party has wound down to a few stragglers and one guitar player outside, Conrad, Sam, and Jack snack on tamales and salsa in the kitchen. A television blares the local evening newscast in the background. The weatherman calls for thunderstorms and lightning over the weekend.

"How about a margarita?" Jack says, emptying his beer bottle and tossing it into a recycling bin near the open door to the back patio. Guitar music drifts in as someone plays a classical Spanish dance.

Conrad peeks outside to see Paulo hop the low wooden fence again, toting a full bottle of tequila. "Paulo's got your poison. Here he is."

"The party goes on, amigos," Paulo says with a grin, entering the kitchen. "I like to keep a case of the stuff for emergencies." Paulo grabs a pitcher of lemon-and-lime mix from the fridge and stirs in an ample amount of tequila and ice.

"You live next door?" Sam says, taking his fresh margarita and squeezing in a lime wedge.

"*Sí.*" Paulo sips his own salted cocktail. "When I moved here a couple years back, I stayed with Ariel and Conrad for a while, looking around. The place next door came up for rent, and I thought, 'Why not stay close to family?'"

Conrad snorts. "A little too close sometimes." He jabs Jack playfully in the ribs, but a menacing undertone causes the joke to fall flat.

Jack eyes Paulo's tattoo of a lovely Latina lady and quickly shifts gears. "*¿Quién es la mujer?*"

Paulo checks out his forearm. Sadness tints his tan face a little. "*Ah, mí amor.* From Columbia. She was killed two years ago this month."

"Oh, I'm sorry, man," Jack replies.

An uncomfortable silence settles in. Jack inspects a photo on the fridge. A young Conrad Bane Sr. sits on a park bench with his lovely young wife, Candy. They look about thirty and wear seventies clothes.

"Look at Candy in this picture! Hot mama!" Jack croaks.

"Yeah, she was a looker back then," Conrad says, leaning against the counter and popping the top on a fresh beer.

Conrad surveys the party through the kitchen window and sees Candy sucking pathetically on her oxygen mask. "She really went downhill after Dad died." He takes a long pull on the bottle. "She finally agreed to move down here. With my brother, Jeff, movin' down this year, she finally budged."

"She lives here . . . with you and Ariel?" Jack asks.

"Says she can't afford to move into her own place," Conrad says and shrugs. "Michelle won't have her at their place." Conrad waves his hand around the small kitchen and open living area. "So, this is it."

"I thought Jack told me that your family was part of the 9/11 survivor settlement?" Sam asks, dipping a chip into a bowl of lukewarm queso.

Conrad snorts, "What a joke. We got a pittance. Bastard lawyers. Some technicality about Pop's service record or somethin'. They're no better than the towel heads that dropped the towers, if you ask me."

Sam nods politely to cover his flinch at the racial slur and stuffs the chip into his mouth.

In the momentary silence, the television news anchor seems exceptionally loud. "In other news, police believe they may have a serial arsonist on their hands. In an incident similar to the Ahzartec fire"—Sam abruptly turns toward the TV images of a burning building—"another office building was nearly burned to the ground this afternoon."

The camera follows a handsome middle-aged politician as he shakes hands with supporters. Red-and-blue signs reading ELECT KYLE BERGEN stick up from the crowd.

"Senator Donald Bergen," the reporter continues, "visiting Charlotte to support his brother's recent election to the House of Representatives, was shocked to find Kyle Bergen's political headquarters on fire upon arriving. . . ."

Emergency workers, firefighters, and police run around a smoldering one-story office building.

Paulo points to the footage of firefighters hosing down the building's smoking black remains. "Hey, that's Station Sixteen. Good guys down there."

"While no one was injured," the reporter concluded, "the fire marshal neither confirmed nor denied the use of a cell phone as an ignition device, which police say might have played a part in last week's—"

Abruptly, the TV goes dark, and the kitchen becomes quiet.

Conrad lays the clicker on the counter and stares at Sam. "It's a party."

20

Sam ducks beneath police tape and takes in the scene. The former headquarters of Kyle Bergen is now a blackened, gutted shell. The remains of the one-story office building still smoke in a few places, and through the open storefront, Sam sees the skeleton of a blackened bathroom near the back of the space. The parking lot is also empty, except for a red-haired police officer eating a burger in his squad car.

"Excuse me," Sam says, startling the officer as he approaches.

The officer swallows hard, wipes his mouth with a fast-food napkin, and holds up the burger. "Long night."

Sam smiles. "I'm sorry. I didn't mean to—"

The officer pulls himself out of the car and shakes Sam's hand. "No worries. Jimmy Prinz." Before Sam can respond, Jimmy looks quizzically at Sam and says, "Do I know you?"

Sam smiles. "You may have seen me before. I'm an investigator."

"That's it," Jimmy says, snapping a finger. "You're working the Ahzartec case, right?"

Sam shakes his head. He looks around. "Where's the fire department?"

"Finished up an hour ago. Left me here to make sure no one tampered with the site until the county fire marshal's office gets here," Jimmy says and hooks his thumb in a pocket.

The gesture reminds Sam of a teenage girl. Of Hannah.

"Jimmy, do you mind if I take a look around?"

"You insure this building too?"

"No," Sam answers honestly.

The officer surveys Sam for a moment and nods for Sam to enter.

"Thanks."

Sam approaches the open frame of what used to be a glass-lined front wall. Large shards of glass lie on the sidewalk, and the blackened innards of the office are now draped with clear plastic sheets. Sam steps inside and takes a closer look.

Partially burnt desks and tables are stacked to one side. Reams of blackened paper, posters, and office supplies create a mountain of dusty debris. He eyes a damaged poster with partial words: ———LE BERGEN: YOUR VOICE FOR FREEDOM ———ING OUR SOLDIERS!

Sam walks about the crime scene for a few moments without any significant findings. As he's about to step back through the open front window to leave, a glint in the corner catches his eye.

Sam checks the parking lot. Jimmy leans against his squad car and slurps his soda dry. He's not paying attention.

Sam crouches and picks up a small silver owl about the size of a bumblebee. It has a small metal ring on its head. He stuffs the charm in his pocket and steps back through the plastic.

"Thanks, Jimmy," Sam says with a wave.

Jimmy holds up a hand in farewell.

21

In a small garden courtyard lit magically with moonlight, Hannah and Travis sign to each other on a wicker love seat. Travis takes Hannah's face in his hands and kisses her gently.

Heading outside for a breath of fresh air, Sam cracks open a beer and stops short when he sees the kids. His pale ale splashes down his front.

"Oh, sorry," Sam says. Sam clumsily signs, "I'm sorry," and wipes down his shirt.

Travis smiles and points to a visible hearing aid in his ear. "It's okay. I have partial hearing."

"Oh, okay. Thanks."

After an awkward silence, Sam gestures inside. "You two want anything to drink? We have soda . . . or milk. . . ."

Hannah and Travis chuckle and shake their heads.

Sam fumbles with his beer cap for a moment and eventually shoves it into a pocket. "Well, it was nice to meet you—"

"Travis."

"Travis, right." Sam nods and turns to his niece. "Hannah, it'll be bedtime soon?"

Hannah nods, almost laughing. She signs something to Sam.

"After warm milk and cookies," he translates. "Very funny. I'm just gonna—" Sam yanks a thumb toward the house. "Travis, nice to meet you. Okeydoke."

Hannah and Travis pick up where they left off.

"I'm a dork," Sam mumbles to himself, takes a long pull on his beer, and closes the patio door behind him.

☙❧

After midnight, Sam sleepily makes his way through the dim living room to the kitchen. He grabs a cup and fills it with cool water from the fridge. As he returns to the living room, he stops with a start and shouts, "Holy shit!"

Hannah is lying on the couch, eyes red, wide awake. She sits up and signs, "Sorry."

He shakes his head. "It's okay. You just startled me."

Sam hesitates but sits next to her on the couch. He pats her knee awkwardly.

Hannah throws her arms around him and begins to wail.

Sam doesn't really know how to react. He puts an arm around his niece and smooths her hair. She starts to calm a little and wipes her runny nose on his pajama top. He chuckles sadly.

In the puffy armchair across from Sam and Hannah, a wisp of moonlight morphs into the form of Alex, unseen by her family.

Sam gently pushes Hannah's shoulders up into a sitting position so she can see his face. He speaks and signs, not sure where the words come from.

"When your mom was little, I used to tease her for being a scaredy-cat. She never wanted to go on the super slide at the mall or the pirate ship at the fair, and it drove me nuts." He signs *carnival* and *scared*.

Hannah shifts a little but listens and wipes her eyes. She focuses on Sam's intermittent signs and reads his lips closely.

"I used to get on her case the most, though, for the tree swing outside our house." Sam extends his left forearm across his body and places his right hand at a right angle, wiggling his fingers like a tree. "Your grandfather put it up one summer and was real proud of it—it had strong ropes and a wooden plank, and it was hung pretty low so you could really get going on the thing.

"One afternoon, I dared Alex to go on the swing, and, as usual, she said no. I called her a chicken and squawked and danced around her until she relented." Sam makes a bird sign and opens the pretend beak with his thumb and finger, the sign for *chicken*. "Finally, she was sick of being made fun of and agreed to go on the swing."

Sam opens his hand near his face and moves it away while closing it. "We went outside—Dad was in the garage or something—and she got on the swing. She was so nervous, I could see her hands shaking, but she was gonna prove me wrong.

"I pushed her high, and still, she didn't cry," he continues, gesturing *high* and *cry*. "But something clicked, and she started liking it; she was like . . . having fun."

Hannah smiles a little at this.

"The thing we didn't realize was that it had stormed hard the night before, and Dad had forgotten to put the swing away like he usually did. It got drenched all night long, and the wood had become weak and started to crack. Well, of course, you know where this is going. . . ."

Hannah nods and signs, "Broken."

Sam nods. "At the highest point in the swing's arc, it cracked and broke." Sam cringes. "As soon as Alex got to where her toes skimmed the leaves, and she could go no higher, right when she began trusting the swing, it broke in half."

Hannah signs, "What did she do?"

"She held on for dear life, screaming all the while, dangling from the ropes, upside down," Sam replies. "I laughed at her, if you can believe it. She was screaming her head off when I finally got her down. From that moment on, she promised herself she would never be afraid again. And she never was."

For a moment, Hannah's face is a watercolor of happiness. She signs, "I just don't know what to do. How to go on." She makes the sign for *walk forward*.

Sam nods at his niece. "I know. Neither do I."

Hannah smiles at her uncle. They sit together on the couch for a while. Eventually Hannah drifts off on one side of the couch. Sam's head lolls back, and his eyes close too. Uncle and niece doze together, two peas in a sad pod.

From across the room, Alex blows them both an invisible kiss.

22

Alex

Things are getting a little better. What I have learned here is like what I learned on prom night. It's better to just lie back and get it over with. *Seriously.* So . . . Big Gray has been bringing people around when I'm in the construction zone. They stand near me, and it gives them something they are missing. The view changes when they're by me, like this one time when Big Gray brought around a skinny man with a bushy beard. His blue uniform reminded me of a Civil War reenactment Sam dragged me to one time outside of Raleigh. When the man adjusted the navy-blue cap, I noticed his pinky was missing on one hand. When the soldier stood near me, I could see through the tarps really clearly. There was a field. I think it was an old farmhouse in the country. There was a young man in overalls—digging a hole, and I could see a well and gravestones nearby. While we were standing there, I felt this force or feeling or *something* flow from the bearded guy next to me. It ran through me like a current and then out through the tarps to the world beyond the tarps. It wasn't my world, but it meant something to the guy next to me. After a minute or two, the soldier closed his eyes and seemed really relieved. I watched him leave then. Never saw him again.

23

Jack and Sam approach the delivery door of Uptown Charlotte's North Carolina Raptor Institute. Jack carries a plastic food container.

Sam pounds on the heavy metal door. A second later, Paulo opens it, wearing a security guard uniform and a grin.

"*Hola*, Paulo!" Jack says. "We come bearing a gift from your cousin."

Jack hands Paulo the container. He opens it and smells chicken enchiladas and steaming beans and rice.

Sam smiles. "Jack dropped off a gift for Conrad's baby today. Ariel insisted we bring you lunch on our way back to the office."

"Ariel is almost as good a cook as Mama was," Paulo replies with a look toward the sky. "*Perdóneme, Mamá*." He beckons the men inside.

Inside the storeroom, the men walk through large stores of feed, plant fertilizer, and shelves of cleaning supplies.

"The center's rescued or rehabilitated more than eleven thousand birds over the last twenty years," says Paulo. "Falcons, eagles, vultures. Over six hundred injured birds arrive for diagnosis each year."

"How many times you repeat that speech in a day?" Jack says with an elbow to Paulo's side.

Paulo smiles. "About a hundred."

The men pass medical facilities where vets treat a wary hawk.

"The fire department doesn't mind you moonlighting here?" Sam asks.

Paulo shakes his head. "Nah. They worked out a schedule for me. Conrad pulled some strings, you know."

Jack smiles. "Good ol' Connie."

Sam stops abruptly as he enters the cavernous atrium. "Whoa," he says and looks up at the enormous glass roof. Large birds of prey perch inside a mile-high sunroom filled with trees and shrubs.

"Wow," Jack parrots. "This is cool." A falcon swoops above his head and lands on a woman's arm nearby. She wears an NC Raptor Institute shirt and elbow-length leather gloves. A few kids gaze openmouthed at the bird.

"The atrium is brand-new," says Paulo. "They rotate the birds in and out, use it for fundraising events."

The men take a seat on a bench near a potted cypress tree.

"In fact," Paulo says, "There's a big event here next month. Lots of high rollers, free food, a band . . .everyone dresses up. It's a lot of fun. You guys should come by."

Jack raises an eyebrow. "Not sure I can afford your lifestyle, Paulo."

Paulo smiles. "I'll be working as an usher. I'll sneak you in for some champagne and a few tunes. That eighties cover band that Ariel likes is playing. She's making Conrad bring her, too, if she's not had the baby yet."

Paulo opens his lunchbox and shares a few homemade chips with Sam and Jack.

"How's Ariel holding up? She's pretty close to popping, isn't she?" Sam asks.

"She sure is," Paulo says with a smile. "I am happy for her but also worried. Things at home can be hard sometimes."

Sam raises his eyebrows. "You mean with the mother-in-law living there full time?"

Paulo's cheeks blush a little. "Yeah. Ariel comes over next door crying sometimes. She's really stressed out trying to deal with Mrs. Bane. She can be a little—"

"She's a pain the ass. Pure and simple," Jack blurts.

Paulo nods at Sam. "It's true. I try to tell Ariel to be patient, but, honestly, I don't know. The stuff she says to Ariel is weird . . . that she took Conrad away from his family . . . and she should quit her job as a nurse to stay home and be a proper wife. I don't know how she'll manage putting up with that and a taking care of a baby. It's a very small house. I offer for Ariel to come over some nights and just hang with me. But it doesn't last long. Conrad wants her home."

"I'm sure she appreciates you trying to help, Paulo," Sam says.

"I think I only make it worse. Mrs. Bane is not my biggest fan."

A brown hawk dives overhead above a high-strung safety net near a group of middle school students on a field trip. The girls in the group squeal and run for their teacher. The boys laugh.

"The kids love this place." Paulo fidgets with the NC Raptor Institute pin on his lapel.

"Are you also a bird lover?" Sam asks.

"Not really." Paulo raises his arm and shows the men the tattoo of the pretty Latina. "But Consuela was a research assistant at the university in Columbia before the accident. Birds of Central America were her specialty. I feel closer to her here, somehow." Paulo stares at the hawk, now circling overhead. Finally, he shakes his head, his gaze shifting down to his shoes.

"Consuela died two years ago," Jack says.

"I'm sorry, Paulo," Sam says. He wants to know more but doesn't push.

Paulo nods his appreciation as his beeper chirps. He checks his pager. "Fire department emergency." Paulo stands to leave and shakes hands with Sam and Jack. "Gotta go. *Lo siento.*" He holds up the container of lunch from Ariel. "Thanks for this!"

Sam and Jack watch Paulo disappear into the storeroom. Above their heads, a large barn owl hoots.

24

"Pit stop?" Jack says, squirming a little on their way out.

"Sure," Sam replies.

In the Raptor Institute's bathroom, Jack pees in the urinal next to Sam. He surveys the bird-themed wallpaper with amusement. Both men zip up. Sam holds his stomach strangely.

"You hungry?" Jack asks.

Sam wavers for a moment and turns toward the stalls but doesn't make it. He hurls all over Jack's loafers.

Jack looks at his shoes in disgust. "Guess not."

Face white, Sam tries to push open a stall door, but it melts beneath his hands. He falls through. Jack enters after him, apparently unaware of the melting door. He picks up Sam, who points toward the sink.

"Water?" Jack says.

Sam shakes his head no. Jack searches the wall. His eyes land on a paper-towel dispenser. Sam nods. Jack yanks a brown paper towel from the roll and hands it to Sam. Sam creates a makeshift desk on Jack's back, pulls a pen from his pocket, and begins to write.

Jack's face reddens in alarm. "What's goin' on, man? You okay?"

Sam continues to scribble on Jack's back without a word.

Unseen by the men, Alex's spirit leans against the wall, pretending to file her nails. She sniffs the scene and crinkles her nose in disgust.

⁂

On the road, Jack drives but constantly looks sideways at Sam, who is now a little less pale.

Sam rests his head on the window, eyes closed. "It's nothing. I just got sick," Sam mumbles.

"Nothing, my extremely fat ass! One minute you're taking a whiz, and the next you're writing the great American novel on my back."

Sam's face reflects the defeat of a man who is cornered. "Take me home, Jack."

"I will. Just as soon as you tell me what in the hell is going on with you."

"I don't know how to describe what's going on with me. I may be having a nervous breakdown," Sam says.

"I thought you were seeing the company shrink," Jack replies.

"I'm not sure Dr. Sheila can really help me here. There's something wrong. Like something really, really wrong with me."

Jack glances at his partner and friend. Sam's pale complexion and dark-circled eyes belie sheer exhaustion. "There's nothing wrong with you, Sam. Remember when my pops passed three years ago? I was a total zombie. Kate had to drag my ass out of bed every morning so I wouldn't dissolve into the sheets."

Sam nods.

"It's normal. Part of grieving. And this is so much more"—Jack struggles to find the word—"intense. Being your sister, man. It was *Alex*. I've never seen a brother and sister as close as you two."

Sam's eyes water, and he peers out the window at the concrete wall dividing a neighborhood from the highway. Sam wants to confide in his best friend, but the words won't come. He wants to tell Jack that, to him, losing Alex feels like someone cut off an arm or reached inside his abdomen and yanked out a vital organ.

"Well, I'm sure you'll figure it out, man," Jack says. "Let me know if I can do anything for you, okay?"

Sam nods. "You can. Just take me home."

25

A week later, Jack approaches Sam's front door. The grass is ankle-high, and a few wilted, wet newspapers lie scattered around the yard.

Jack knocks. No answer. He peeks through the window and sees a mess—whiskey bottles, pizza boxes, files, the works—strewn across the coffee table.

Jack sighs. "Jesus H. Christ on a stick." He trots to the garage and peers in a window. Sam's black SUV is there, silent and cold.

Jack knocks on the front door again.

Inside his bedroom, Sam hears the pounding and Jack's muffled voice: "I know you're in there, Sam. Open up or I'll take a dump on your lawn."

Sam covers his head with a pillow.

Defeated, Jack retreats to his car with a knitted brow. He makes yet another phone call and leaves his third message for the day. "Doctor Sheila is looking for you, Sam. You missed your appointment. Gimme a call, buddy."

He cranks his classic muscle car and drives away.

26

In his study, Sam sits at his desk. His crisp white collar and designer tie droop with sweat. Sam's writing hand shakes in resistance to an unseen force. The pen, with a mind of its own, painfully scrawls out a recipe for cornbread.

When he's finished, Sam wipes his brow with a wrist. Sweat glistens on his forehead. He stares at the letter he's just written, unsure what to do next. After a few moments, he opens his small trash can and drops the cornbread letter into the bin. He releases the foot pedal, and the metal lid closes with a clang.

Outside, in the hallway, Hannah watches, unseen, through the open study door. As Sam looks up, she retreats down the hall, hoisting her school book bag over her shoulder.

Sam starts to follow, but meanders into the living room instead. He notices a half-full cardboard box marked *Alex's Stuff* and tosses a lone sparkly earring and some papers into a garbage bag nearby. He rifles through the box, trying on a pair of 3-D glasses, shuffling through random personal items, and stopping at a purple business card that sways in

3-D. Sam flips the card over. Written in fluid cursive are the words *For Sammy.*

ೲ

Sam looks from the purple business card to a funky purple house. A white wooden sign in the shape of a hand, palm out, reads MADAME AMANDA, PSYCHIC IRIDOLOGIST & SPIRITUAL COUNSELOR.

Sam looks around him in irrational embarrassment. Traffic whizzes by at the start of evening rush hour. He takes a deep breath and approaches the front door. He knocks. No answer.

He knocks again. This time he turns the door handle, and, with little force, it swings open, hitting the wall with a bang. Sam winces.

"Sorry!" he calls down the hallway to . . . whoever.

"Just a sec!" a woman's voice yells back.

Sam surveys the reading room around him. A playpen filled with baby toys is out of place among the traditional psychic fare—velvet curtain–laden windows, crude wooden masks, and a crystal ball.

Madame Amanda finally enters, wrapping a long scarf around bleached-blonde hair. She squeezes her pregnant belly behind the small table where Sam waits.

"Hey there. Sorry, I'm runnin' behind. When you called, I rushed home from the beauty shop," Amanda says with a twang. She smiles.

Sam is taken aback by her youth and simple beauty.

"Beauty shop?" he asks.

"Well, this readin' room was supposed to belong to Darlene, my sister. My mama had 'the gift of sight' and thought it would pass to Darlene. That girl can't read 'stop' on a stop sign, let alone palms. So, after my first three babies, Mama retired, and I took over. I still work two days a week over at the beauty shop, though."

Sam fidgets uncomfortably. "Right. Well, as I said on the phone, I wanted to talk to you about my sister, Alex."

Madame Amanda smiles widely. "Oh, yes. Lady Alex. She was one of my best customers."

Sam knits his brow. He notices he's doing a lot of that lately. Frowning—at pretty much everything. He makes an attempt to relax his face.

"Lady Alex?" he asks, voice squeaking a little. He clears his throat self-consciously.

Amanda laughs. "Oh, that was just a funny nickname I gave her on account of her past life in the royal court o' England."

Sam smiles and shakes his head. For a moment, he's overcome with a feeling. Nothing specific, really, but just a nudge, like Alex poking him from behind. He turns his head and looks around the room, a bit frantic.

"I'd say she's coming along for the ride today, then?" Amanda asks.

Sam whips his head back around. "What? What do you mean?"

Amanda looks long into Sam's eyes. "I think she's here," she says evenly.

"I don't know . . . about any of this really. It's just that it's been hard . . . since she's been gone. And there's some things going on with me. And I don't really buy them. But they are happening to me, so I know they are—that it's—um . . . Sorry." Sam sighs, a bit defeated.

Amanda takes a deep breath. "It's okay, Sam. I know this ain't your cup o' tea."

Sam relaxes a bit.

"Let me tell you a little about Alex, then," Amanda says, placing her palms facedown on the reading table. "Your sister was a regular. Five years or so. I saw her at least once a month. She's a firecracker, that one. A lot of people will miss her, I believe."

Sam smiles and uncomfortably nods in agreement. "I'm investigating her death," Sam says after a quiet minute.

Madame Amanda lights a bundle of sage and begins cleansing Sam and the room.

"Really? Aren't the police doing that?" Amanda says, waving the burning sage around Sam's head.

Sam coughs. "Not a very good job of it."

Amanda smiles lightly. "Hmmm . . ." She snuffs out the sage bundle in a nearby ashtray. The sweet fumes linger.

"Do you have any information that might help me? Alex wrote my name on the back of your card." Sam hands Amanda the purple business card.

She flips it over and reads Alex's words: *For Sammy.* "Maybe she thought we should talk."

"That's why I'm here. Do you know anything about the arson at the Ahzartec building? My sister was covering a story there the day of the fire."

Madame Amanda surveys Sam like a circuit court judge about to bestow a life sentence on a guilty man. Unexpectedly, she blows a huge bubble with her gum and pops it. Sam didn't even know she was chewing gum.

A carved wooden mask stares at Sam from the wall. Madame Amanda looks down toward her feet. "Now I told you, Lincoln, not to bother Mommy when she's giving readings. Go on, now, git on back to the TV."

Sam stands and looks across the table. A toddler holds his mother's multicolored skirt and sucks a bottle. Sam is taken aback. He also didn't realize there was a kid in the room.

Lincoln takes a long pull on his bottle and scuttles away. Sam watches him go into the nearby room with the playpen and plop down on his diaper like a bean bag in front the TV. A silent cartoon plays on the screen.

Alarmingly, Madame Amanda stands, reaches over the table, and grabs Sam's head in a viselike grip. Eyeball to eyeball, Amanda stares into his right eye.

Sam is paralyzed as tiny eagles seem to flood from his eye into hers. Instinctively, he pulls back. "What the hell are you doing!?" Sam sputters.

Amanda plops back into her chair and rubs her big belly. "How long have you been writing?"

Sam looks incredulously at her.

Madame Amanda stares him down. "I'd say it's happened more than once, according to those gorgeous eyeballs of yours," she says.

Sam is shocked and frazzled. "I think I better get going. . . ."

"Every disturbance, every change in a person's life, is all represented in the iris of the eye. Ancients called it the 'mirror of the soul.' Mama called it the 'art of readin' eyes.'"

"This is crazy. You're . . . you're a crazy person!" Sam shouts as he heads for the front door.

Amanda continues, undeterred. "My feelin' is that you and Alex are forever connected on the soul plane. Whatever's happening to you is because of this connection. Alex is still tied to this world and can't move on until somethin' is resolved."

Sam stops in his tracks. He turns to face Madame Amanda.

"What isn't resolved? Her death?"

"Dunno. Don't see that."

"Then how will I know what to do?" Sam asks, shaken. He stands in the open doorway.

Madame Amanda gazes at Sam for a long minute. "You'll know." Madame Amanda pushes herself up heavily from the table. "Nice meetin' you, Sam."

"But how will I know?" Sam repeats.

Madame Amanda pops her gum loudly. "Just take a look around, sweetie. There are signs all around you."

27

A huge neon sign—*LIQUOR-BEER-WINE*—shines bright blue in the night. Sam exits the building, brown bag in hand, and unlocks his car with a chirp.

"Now *that's* a sign," he mutters to himself, gets in the car, and drives away.

୬୦

At home, Sam moves down the hall toward the only light in the house—in his study. Sam enters to find Hannah rummaging through the wastebasket.

The heat rises in Sam's cheeks. "Hannah, what are you doing?"

Hannah ignores him. She clutches blue papers in one hand and digs through the trash with the other.

Sam yells, "What in the hell do you think you are doing?"

Hannah ignores him again.

He takes a deep breath and remembers that Hannah can't hear him. A little too roughly, he pulls Hannah's shoulder, twisting her around.

Hannah, shocked, pulls away.

Sam notices his own preprinted envelopes in her hand and snaps, "What are you doing?"

Hannah shrugs and turns away. She finds the letter she's searching for in the bin. It's spells out a recipe for cornbread in small, cursive writing on Sam's blue stationery paper.

Sam clasps her face with both hands and turns it to face his. "Did you mail the last one?"

Hannah nods yes.

Sam yanks the letter from her hand, rips it to shreds, and stuffs the remnants into the trash can. Sam points to his mouth and speaks deliberately. "It is not okay to go digging through other people's trash. Do you want more crazies paying us a visit?"

Hannah stares at the trash can.

Sam grabs Hannah by the shoulders and shakes her. "Are you listening?"

Hannah ignores his pleas and reaches into the trash can. She pulls out the letter, totally intact. She holds the fully formed letter by her fingertips.

Sam and Hannah both freeze and stare at the letter.

After a moment, Sam grabs the letter and again, rips it to shreds, dropping the strips into the trash can with satisfaction.

Hannah tips the can toward her and looks up at Sam. Her face tells the story. Sam reaches into the trash can and pulls out the fully restored letter.

Sam shouts, "I've had enough, goddamn it!"

Sam rummages through his desk, pulls out a lighter, and torches the letter. The paper burns. Sam barely conceals his fury.

Clear flames engulf the letter as Sam holds it over the waste basket, the dancing tongues masking the handwritten signature that reads *Love, Grandma Britt.* He feels no pain as the flames lick his wrists.

"Alex certainly broke plenty of rules in her day, but I expected more from you. I always thought you at least had a brain, a head on your shoulders that wasn't as wild and . . . and . . . insane as your mother's—"

Sam stops speaking. Hannah stares wide-eyed at the burning letter. Flames now engulf the paper and Sam's entire hand and arm.

Sam jerks back and drops the letter onto the floor.

"Are you okay?" Hannah says, her consonants rounded.

Sam looks incredulously at his hand and cuff, which remain unsinged while glowing in the white flame. Sam simply blows it out.

He looks at Hannah. "No. I am not okay."

The letter burns white on the floor, unharmed. Sam and Hannah look at each other and simultaneously begin stomping out the flames.

Hannah picks up the letter. Good as new. She hands the letter to Sam and signs to him.

"The eagle says to mail it? What the hell is that supposed to mean?" Sam snaps.

Hannah runs from the room and returns with two new eagle paintings—one orange, one purple.

"I can't get this image out of my head," she says, holding up a painting in each hand.

Sam shakes the letter in rebellion. "I am not mailing this! Look what happened the last time! I got attacked. What if I hadn't been home? What if that man had hurt you?"

Hannah pushes the eagles toward him. He throws them to the ground, cracking one of the frames.

"I'm not mailing this!" He drops the letter into the trash can.

Hannah and Sam stand face-to-face in a standoff. Nobody moves. After a moment, Sam sighs heavily.

Hannah points to his hand. Sam looks down to see the letter back in his hand. He eyes it, defeated.

∞

Outside their front door, Hannah watches as Sam huffs to the curb in the moonlight, shoves the letter into the mailbox, and violently throws up the red flag. In the corner of the front porch, Alex's spirit gives her daughter a thumbs-up.

28

Alex

Big Gray has been really getting on my last nerve. He's really pushy. I told him I just want to watch my brother and my daughter and not be dragged into all his people's various bullshit requests, but he won't budge. He also tells me I will be forever stuck here, near the construction zone, if I don't help my family make right what happened to me.

Truthfully, I don't remember what happened to me. It's a blur of images. I recall going to the office building for that terrorist protest, and I was really jazzed because they finally gave me a chance to write something other than puppy-saves-baby-from-burning-trailer stories. And I remember I had a lot of great ideas on how to position the article. That company, Ahzartec, is owned by a Saudi billionaire with known ties to terror organizations in the Middle East. Yet they are given tax breaks by our government for providing "funding" for alternative energy sources here in the US—all while providing cheap crude-oil products to American companies. Something stinks in suburbia.

The protestors are no better—they will use any medium to get their messages across about how much they hate the US government for allowing foreign ownership of US subsidiaries or whatever the cause of the moment is. So, I was going to write a great story. But instead, I'm here playing telephone with a bunch of ghosts. Speaking of which, there's a little girl here tugging on my sleeve. Apparently, she really needs to tell me something. Duty calls.

29

Jack pounds on Sam's front door.

"Abernethy! Boss or not, I'm not leaving here until you open this door! I mean it!" he yells.

The door opens. Sam smirks at his friend and shades his eyes from the sunlight. His bed head and shadowed beard complement his wrinkled pajamas.

"Jesus, Sam, what in the hell is going on? You haven't been to work for a week"—Jack looks behind Sam at the pile of trash on the coffee table—"and you're holed up in here like some loser frat boy on meth! Seriously."

"Gimme five minutes." Sam grunts and disappears into the house.

❧

Sam and Jack drink in a corner of their go-to Irish pub uptown.

"It's been happening for a couple of months. Since Alex died. Something comes over me. I can't control it." Sam takes a pull on his pint of dark beer.

Jack considers this. "Like in the bathroom the other day?"

Sam nods. "I can feel this—I don't know—force or something, and it really wants to write. And when it does, my hand moves, and I can't stop it."

Jack stretches his back. Sam can see he's uncomfortable.

"Have you told Dr. Sheila?" Jack asks.

"Not exactly, but kind of. I mean, how in the hell am I supposed to describe this to a sane person?" Sam replies.

"Are you saying I am not sane?" Jack smiles and gulps his lager.

"I talked to my GP a little. I don't want the company knowing *anything* about this."

"What did your regular doc say?" Jack asks.

"I asked her about alien hand syndrome."

"What the hell is that?"

Sam adjusts his bar stool. "Super rare disorder. If the right hand tucks in your shirt, your left hand pulls it out—something like that."

"So can your alien hand—you know . . ." Jack mimics jerking off with a lewd grin.

Sam laughs hard. "Uh, that would be no."

"Maybe it's psychological," Jack says. "They'll give you a couple good prescriptions—clear it right up."

The waitress appears with a basket of hushpuppies and fries. "Here's your heart attack, boys, extra crispy," says Brittany.

"Thanks, doll," Jack says, digging in and moaning with delight at the fried wonders.

Brittany jabs a thumb at Jack and says to Sam, "Get this guy some help."

Sam chuckles. "Believe me, I've tried."

As Brittany takes her leave and returns to the bar, which is nearly empty in the workday afternoon, Sam pulls a paper towel from his jacket pocket and lays it flat on the table. "Look at this. It's not even my handwriting."

Jack scans the jagged-edged paper towel that had once been on his back in the restroom of the Raptor Institute. He shivers at the strange memory.

"The family Jackson . . . a road called Blue Holly . . . the town of Statesville in the northern part of Carolina," Jack reads. "If you're Melvin's kin, your future and my past await you. My debt was repaid but got lost along the way. I've been told it lies fifty paces north of the old well, dead center between the stones of Hank and Hezekiah. Use it well, and I am free. —Earl"

Sam downs the rest of his beer. "See what I mean?"

"Who the hell is Melvin Jackson?" Jack asks, handing the paper towel back to Sam.

Sam folds it carefully and returns it to his pocket. "I have no idea."

⚬⚬

On the darkened street in front of Sam's house, Jack pulls to a stop. Sam hops out.

Jack cracks the window. "Go see Sara."

Sam ducks down to meet Jack's gaze. "No."

"She might be able to help. You need to talk to someone."

"'Night, Jack." Sam heads for his front door, raises a hand in goodbye, and does not look back.

30

"I'm sorry, Mr. Abernethy, Mr. Beck. . . . I told them you were in a meeting," Dina, the grandmotherly front-desk administrator, says quickly as a couple pushes their way past her into Sam's office.

A middle-aged man in jeans and a western-style shirt rounds the desk and gives Jack a bear hug. "Mr. Abernethy, I'm Ryan Jackson. My wife, Lana, and I can't thank you enough for what you done."

"Whoa, Nelly." Jack politely extricates himself from the man's grip. Jack points to Sam. "He's your man."

Sam shoots an eye at Jack, stands, and extends a hand. "Hello, Mr. Jackson. I'm Sam Abernethy."

The plump woman next to Ryan squeals and bounces on the balls of her ballet slippers. She wears a flowing dress in muted tones and has a long braid down her back, as if she's just walked in from the prairie. "We just wanted to thank you in person, Mr. Sam," Lana Jackson says sweetly.

Sam shrugs. "You got me. I'm stumped."

Ryan holds up an envelope and says, "Your daughter let us know where to find you."

A look of recognition slides over Sam's face, and he exchanges a look with Jack. "Hannah."

Jack looks confused.

Lana digs into a weathered brown leather shoulder bag and removes the bathroom paper-towel letter from a light blue envelope. Sam's stationery. With his address on it.

Damn, he thinks. "She must've mailed the letter," Sam mutters. "Again."

"The letter from the bathroom? How did she—why?" Jack asks.

"Because the eagle told her to." Sam shakes his head. "I'll explain later."

Jack nods his head. "Right."

Lana raises a hand, like a child in class. Sam encourages her to speak. "We've been waiting years, really, for a sign like this."

Sam takes a deep breath. "A sign?"

☙

In a field about fifty yards from a weathered but well-kept farmhouse, Jack, Sam, Lana, and Ryan stand looking over a hole in the ground as large as a mid-sized car. The hole is flanked by an old stone well permanently covered with wood planks and a giant oak tree. Crumbling headstones stand on either side of the pit.

Lana dabs a tear from her eye.

Ryan beams. "My great-grandfather, Hezekiah Jackson, told a tale of his grandmother, Beulah, the wife of a Confederate soldier that disappeared during the Civil War. Beulah waited day after day for her husband, Melvin Jackson, to return safely home, but she never received any word or letter about his fate."

Lana touches her husband's arm and picks up the narrative that had clearly been told time and time again. "Years later, just after the war ended, Beulah received a surprise visit from a thin man wearing a Union soldier's cap. He had a missing pinky. The man's name was Earl, and he told Beulah that Melvin had saved his life during the war. He wanted to pay back Melvin's family for the kindness that Melvin had shown him on the battlefield. Injured and at the wrong end of Melvin's bayonet, Earl had pleaded to be spared for the sake of his three daughters. Melvin took pity on the man and captured instead of killed him."

Ryan nods enthusiastically. "On the ride to the Confederate prisoner of war camp, Melvin told Earl about his one last desire—to return to his young son, Hank, and wife, Beulah, on their farm near Statesville, North Carolina." Ryan pauses for breath. "Of course, Melvin never made it back to his family or his farm."

Ryan points to a dirt-covered ancient wooden chest they'd dug out of the hole. "Before Earl took his leave the day he visited Beulah, he unloaded this from his wagon."

Sam and Jack, mouths agape, stare at an ancient wooden chest with its lid open. Years of dirt and grime cover mounds of gold coins, ribbons of Confederate and Union cash, and a stack of old letters, crumbling but still intact and tied with a faded red velvet bow, now black in places with mold and age.

"Even we didn't believe the old legend until your letter came, Mr. Abernethy," Ryan says. "The story went that Beulah was so petrified that Union forces would come to reclaim the treasure, she had her son, Hank, bury it in a secret location for safekeeping."

Lana, lovely and plain as the sinking sun, clasps her hands in joy. "But after Hank, now father to little Hezekiah, died suddenly from the Spanish flu, all trace of the treasure's location disappeared with him." Lana jerks a thumb at Ryan and smiles. "His people been diggin' up this property for years." She smiles and waves a hand broadly to indicate the fields past the farmhouse, now planted with soybeans. "Your letter finally told us where to dig. It's a miracle!"

Sam takes a deep breath and stares into the setting sun for a moment, silent and confused. The whole experience feels like a black ink spot on his brain, spreading rapidly across tissue paper.

Ryan clutches Sam's shoulder. "How did you do this? How can we ever repay you?"

"Well, I think ten percent ought to cover it," Jack pipes in.

Sam cuts Jack off with a look. "I don't want money, Mr. and Mrs. Jackson. But there is one thing you could do for me. If you don't mind."

Ryan smiles warmly. "Anything."

31

Back on the road, Jack inspects a plastic bag holding a crumbling piece of yellowed parchment. The ink is faded to gray, and the edges of the old letter are jagged with sections missing, victim to decay and bugs.

"Get a department analyst to look at it," Sam says. "I want to see if the handwriting in the letter from the chest matches the paper-towel letter. Need to understand if there's some connection here that's real."

"Well, that treasure chest sure looked pretty damn real to me!" Jack snorts. "If you think about it . . . this is actually . . . right up Sara's alley."

Sam shoots him a withering look and shakes his head. "Get that new guy we just hired—what's his name?"

"Sara is the best analyst the department ever had. And she was your sister's best friend. Just talk to her."

"There's a reason Sara and I broke up," Sam says, extending a hand to flip on the radio.

Jack gazes out the window at farmland fading with the sunset. He mutters, "Yeah. You."

A moment of silence settles between them as farmlands roll by.

Jack tries one last time. "Just think about it. It would be good for you."

Sam sighs heavily. "I'm not going to see Sara, Jack." Sam repeats, shaking his head. "Not in a million years."

32

The university's criminal justice building always reminded Sam of an institution: gray, rectangular, tiny slits for windows. He never liked coming here, even when he was a student. One criminology class was enough to dissuade him from pursuing law school, so he went to business school instead. Ironically, he ended up in investigations anyway.

In the foyer outside Sara's office, Sam reads the brass sign:

SARA PARKER, PhD

FORENSIC HANDWRITING ANALYSIS

CRIMINAL JUSTICE DEPARTMENT

He takes a seat in the small waiting area next to a young student rifling through her purse. The nerdy-looking girl pulls out lip balm and applies it thickly. Sam can smell the cherry flavor.

"She's a really good professor, don't you think?" the student says.

It takes Sam a second to realize she's talking to him. He smiles politely and says, "Excuse me?"

The young lady smacks her well-oiled lips. "I like Dr. Parker a lot, don't you? She's really good."

"Oh," Sam replies. "I'm not a student."

The student hugs a stack of books and smiles at Sam. "Oh . . . we were wondering if Professor Parker had a boyfriend." The girl beams with interest.

Sam feels a little self-conscious and stutters, "No, I work—used to work—with Sara. With the professor."

The student loses her smile and surveys Sam critically. "Are you a cop? There was a cop in here the other day."

"No." Sam waits for a follow-up, but the student stares on.

"Yeah," she says after a long moment looking him up and down unabashedly through gold metal-rimmed glasses. "Dr. Parker works on a lot of fraud cases."

Sam nods, and the girl returns to her stack of books. She flips through a psychology text.

"Are you a psych student?" Sam says with a nod to the heavy book.

The girl lights up and nods. "Criminal psych."

Sam leans in a bit. "Well, actually, I've been having a problem. Maybe you can help me."

The girl nods with interest.

"I have these episodes—I guess you call them—where I get nauseous and write letters. But the letters are in other people's handwriting. Mostly dead people, I think." Sam breathes a sigh of relief. He has said the truth.

The girl stares thoughtfully at Sam for a long minute. Sam looks hopefully back at her. Next moment, she gathers her books, stands abruptly, and hurries down the hallway without a word.

Inside her office, Sara Parker examines the parchment letter from the old chest and the paper-towel letter side by side. Sporting rimless spectacles and loose nut-brown hair, Sara has the fresh look of a student rather than a tenured professor.

"You can see here"—she points to words in each letter—"the peaks on the letter *m* are both very high. The *a*'s and *o*'s are open on both . . . and look at the way the *t* loops on each sample. That's a really specific marker."

Sam watches Sara push a stray lock of hair behind an ear.

"I'll need more time, but at first blush, I'd say they could be a match," she concludes.

Sam is jolted back to reality.

"That's great. Thanks, Sara. I appreciate your help on this."

Sara's attention remains on the samples. "Sam, where'd you get these?" She holds the parchment up to the light. "This looks like it's at least a hundred years old."

"A hundred and fifty, actually. It's from the Civil War," he says, eyeing the parchment from the Jacksons' buried treasure chest.

"Is this part of an investigation?" Sara asks and sticks her glasses atop her head. She carefully appraises Sam.

He bounces on the balls of his feet, uncharacteristically fidgety. "Sort of," he says. "But not through Adelaar."

Sara bites her lip. The weight of a thousand thoughts fills the air between them. Sara is unable to hold in her emotions. She stares at her office wall, and, as she does, her eyes brim with tears. "I miss Alex, Sam."

Sam can't meet her eye.

"I don't know how to manage the fact that we'd just reconnected after so long." Sara grabs a tissue from a box on her desk.

"I was hopeful we could find our way—to something new. Things were strained when you and I—when it didn't work out. She didn't quite know how to *be* between the two of us."

Sam swallows hard and nods indistinctly.

Sara wipes her eyes. "How's Hannah?"

Sam smiles weakly. "A teenager, you know." He swallows back a hard lump forming in his throat.

Sara reaches a hand toward Sam's arm. "If you ever need to talk—"

"Thanks," Sam says. He collects the letters and disappears through the open door.

Sara stares after him.

33

In the living room, Hannah sleeps facedown on the floor in front of the silent closed-captioned television. As Sam drowsily watches from the couch, Hannah's sleeping form morphs into Alex, floating facedown in a swimming pool. Sam, wearing a state college sweatshirt, approaches the blue water and yells to his sister, "Alex! Get up. Quit messing around."

Alex doesn't move a muscle. Sam surveys her wearily. *Nice try.*

"Get your fat ass out of the pool, Alex! Mom's bitching about the turkey getting cold. Let's go."

Sam pokes at her with the pool skimmer. Alex still doesn't stir.

The color drains from his face. Sam jumps in the water after his sister. He pulls her up. She is limp and not breathing. He throws her poolside and shakes her, turning her head to the side and preparing for chest compressions.

Alex giggles as Sam's hands approach her ribs. Sam stops and looks incredulously at Alex as she opens her eyes. She laughs.

"You . . . crazy . . ." Sam growls in frustration, picks her up, and throws her in the pool.

Alex laughs riotously at him. He cannonballs in after her.

Alex's laughter echoes as Sam stirs from his nap spot on the couch. Back in the living world, he picks up a sleeping Hannah and carries her out of the room past three new paintings of bald eagles in blue, black, and green.

☙❧

Sam returns, collects the paintings, and deposits them into a closet filled with at least fifteen others just like them. Behind him, Alex's spirit beams with pride.

34

Alex

I'm happy today. I felt a strange sense of accomplishment when that couple visited Sam and they dug up the treasure chest—like a story that was missing an ending finally came to a satisfying conclusion. I could feel my spirit lift right along with Sam's. I always could tell when something was bothering him. If he was sad, I picked up on it instantly and did whatever I could to make him laugh again. He did have it harder than me, being the oldest and having to take care of all the tough stuff after Mom and Dad were gone. And I always let him. I made it harder on him, in fact. Sometimes I feel bad for that. I hope he knows that I didn't mean to. I was just young and effed up.

Anyway, the tarps at the construction zone are flowing today, and all I can see are eagles, falcons, hawks, and owls. They float and fly in circles over the city. My old city. Where Sam and Hannah live and move about their lives. I send the eagles to Hannah. She always loved big birds of prey as a kid. I send her the eagles so she'll remember that summer I took her to the summer camp at the Raptor Institute. She would come home squealing with delight at having helped the staff there to care for the injured birds in the center. They were really good to her, and that wasn't always the case with other schools, summer camps. Sometimes kids can be mean to anyone that's different. But the center was fantastic. They actually had a staff member who knew sign language, and there were two other kids from the School for the Deaf in Hannah's group. Those were happy days for us.

I know you want to ask, so I will just tell you. There's no sense of missing anyone here. You want me to tell you I miss Hannah, and my heart breaks every time I see her, but it's not true. I feel only joy. Pure and simple. And so, I send her the eagles.

35

A hawk lands atop the Queen City Hotel in downtown Charlotte. The stately building's art deco styling is illuminated only by dim lobby lighting and a nearby streetlamp. In the basement utility room, a gloved hand turns the large main water-supply valve off.

Moments later, a heavy boot steps onto the carpeted hallway of the sixth floor. A clear liquid bubbles around the rubber sole of the heavy boot. A match flares white, lighting a carton of generic cigarettes on fire. The fiery box is dropped onto the soaked carpet. The emergency-exit door swings open and shut. The owner of the boots bars the door shut from the stair side with a metal security bar. Flames shoot from under the stairway door as the boots retreat.

Sam bolts from his dream. *Or was it?*

He rushes to the bathroom and vomits. After a few moments recovering on the bathroom floor, Sam wipes his mouth and looks up to see a message written in shaving cream on the bathroom mirror.

queen city hotel floor 6 no water cigs

Sam looks down at his hand, realizing he's clutching a can of shaving cream. He throws the can back into a drawer and turns to find his phone.

Before he can move, however, the overwhelming scent of paint thinner fills his nostrils. His eyes water and he screws them shut, choking violently.

After a moment, the spasm subsides, and he opens his eyes. His reflection in the mirror sucks in fresh air and—to Sam's shock—exhales a cloud of smoke.

Alex's spirit blows a kiss to herself in the mirror as Sam rushes from the room.

36

The hotel is on fire. Medics escort an old couple across the lawn as two firefighters knock flames from the historic building with a powerful serpentine hose, sending billowing black smoke into the sky. First responders attend to the injured, which include a number of children. Police tape surrounds the building's lobby and front-door area.

Sam runs toward the building from the parking garage. He stares wild-eyed at the burning hotel. *Jesus.*

Sam navigates the mayhem and ducks under the police tape to approach Detective Kelly, a grizzled throwback to the way cops used to be. The detective converses with Arnold Noble, a towering African American senior investigator from the county fire marshal's office. Both men are in good shape, with slightly protruding midsections that belie their middle age.

"It's possible the carpet rolls came into contact with exposed wiring from the remodeling," Arnold says to Detective Kelly.

"Excuse, me, Detective, I need to speak to you," Sam breaks in. His hair and eyes are wild, as if he's stumbled onto the scene from a nearby bar.

The detective gives Sam the once-over, ignores him, and returns to his conversation with Investigator Noble. "The manager claims the construction materials were moved from six to the basement this afternoon. They had the entire sixth floor rented by one"—he checks his notebook—"Jacquard Collique."

"Excuse me," Sam pants, still winded from his run from the car. "I'm the one who called 911."

The men continue speaking as if Sam isn't present.

A young red-haired officer approaches and hands a clipboard to Detective Kelly. "Here's the guest list from floor seven. Jacquard Collique is the managing partner of Collique & Partners, New York."

"Thanks, Jimmy," the detective says, scanning the document.

Sam does a double take when he hears the freckled officer's name. He recognizes the young man from his late-night visit to Senator Bergen's burnt-out office building. Sam wonders if Jimmy remembers him. He shoves that thought aside and blurts, "The sixth floor." He pants and catches his breath. "You need to check the sixth floor for accelerants. Something is wrong on the sixth floor. And there's something about the water."

Finally, all three men stare at Sam.

Detective Kelly looks up from the clipboard. "That's an interesting comment. We'd be happy to take your statement at the police station tomorrow."

"When the fire department arrived, they found the main water supply shut off," Jimmy says to Sam, acknowledging him with a nod.

Sam's face melts with realization. "No sprinklers."

Detective Kelly looks Sam in the eye. "That's right. No sprinklers." He turns to Jimmy. "Why would this law firm rent out the sixth floor if it was being remodeled?"

"Mr. Collique and his firm deal with death threats on a daily basis due to the nature of their cases, sir. They arranged it with the manager. Didn't even want the hotel staff to know where they were staying. But the lawyers never showed. They were called to Washington on an urgent matter this afternoon."

Sam sees a familiar face run by. It takes him a few seconds to register the man in his fire suit. *Paulo.* He and a fellow firefighter carry an injured child on a gurney toward the bank of ambulances near the street. The boy wears an oxygen mask, and blood seeps from a cut on his arm.

"I thought you said there was no one on the sixth floor," Sam says, panic rising.

"Six was vacant, but with no sprinklers, the fire spread to seven before the department could respond," Investigator Noble offers. "The hotel had donated the seventh floor to a kids' summer camp leaving for the mountains tomorrow morning."

Sam is ashen. "Check the sixth floor. The subfloor is soaked. Test for accelerants. Maybe paint thinner or turpentine."

All three men stare at Sam.

"You said they were remodeling, right? I've seen this type of arson on the job. The ignition may have been cigarettes. A pack. Or maybe a carton. Just check the goddamn sixth floor!" Sam yells.

The detective nods to Jimmy, who takes Sam by the arm. "Time to go."

Suddenly, a large window ledge falls from the building and explodes into dust. Noble runs toward the fray.

Jimmy releases Sam near the parking garage and warns, "Stay here."

As Jimmy runs back toward the hotel, Sam looks up to see a body dangling from the remains of the ledge. It's a small girl. She screams. Black smoke pours out behind her from the gaping hole.

A firefighter climbs the ladder toward her. In a moment where the spotlight catches the man's face, Sam sees it is Conrad Jr. in full fire gear. He almost topples over on the rising ladder as it connects with the building but holds tight. The girl loses her grip and slips. A chorus of voices on the ground scream involuntarily, but, at the last second, Conrad grabs the falling girl by the jacket. She swings into the ladder and clutches Conrad's leg.

Sam collapses to the ground in relief.

⁖

An hour later, Jimmy returns to Sam, who sits with his back against the cement wall of the parking garage.

"Everyone's out," Jimmy says, clipboard in hand. "You okay, Mr. Abernethy?"

Sam looks up at Jimmy. "You remembered."

Jimmy nods. "The detective wants you to come downtown tomorrow for a full statement."

Sam nods, exhausted.

Jimmy eyes Sam with compassion. "I won't mention our dinner date the other night." He waits a beat. "Not sure your little unauthorized visit would bode well for either of us."

Sam nods in agreement.

"How's the little girl? Were all the kids okay?" Sam asks, getting to his feet.

"Yeah, a few are being treated for minor cuts and smoke inhalation, but, thank God, they are all alive. Conrad will be up for a medal for that one," Jimmy says with a smile. "And I'm sure Arnold Noble will never hear the end of it."

Sam looks puzzled. "You know Conrad Bane?" Sam shakes his head. "Small world around here."

Jimmy nods. "Guys on the job go to the same watering holes, you know." Jimmy wedges his clipboard under one arm. "I don't know him well, but I get the idea that Conrad isn't all that popular with the other guys. He brags a lot and throws his pedigree around. NYFD and all. His pop was a 9/11 hero or something," Jimmy says, stowing the pen in his uniform pocket.

Sam nods. "Interesting. I don't know him well, but my partner, Jack, does."

"Partner?"

"I call him that," Sam says, "but really we just work together at Adelaar."

Jimmy nods. "We'll be in touch, Mr. Abernethy." Jimmy walks out of the garage back toward the waning lights of the emergency vehicles but turns back. "So . . . how *did* you know? About the cigarettes?"

Sam's eyes light up. "You found them?"

Jimmy nods. "Fragments. Probably a carton."

"It's a little hard to explain," Sam says.

"They're gonna want an explanation tomorrow," Jimmy says. "You know that."

Sam sighs. "Yes."

"If you need any help tomorrow, give me a call." Jimmy reaches into his pocket and pulls out a business card.

Sam's surprise that the officer even has a business card is cut short by a silver flash and a jingle of metal. Sam bends to pick up the small object.

"Found it outside the lobby earlier," Jimmy says. "I meant to show the detective but must've forgot with all the—" He gestures toward the still-smoking high-rise.

Before handing it back to Jimmy, Sam stares at the tiny charm in his palm for a long moment. A silver falcon.

37

Alex

This time it was different. Not like before, when I was spending some quality time at the construction zone, watching Hannah paint. Then, I was overcome by the warm, amazing, buttery smell of fresh cornbread. It was like nothing I had ever smelled before. I saw the ingredients right in front of me—a young woman was frantically searching for the recipe and couldn't find it among a ton of moving boxes. I looked over my shoulder, and a really old lady wearing a shawl was waving at me. She had a perfectly coifed head of red hair. So, I sent the recipe down through the tarps to the searching lady. But I think it was Sam that got it. Not sure why it works that way exactly, but whatever. Hannah ended up sending it to the lady, and she was so happy. Afterwards, I felt full—like I'd eaten an entire pan of that cornbread. It was awesome. The old lady left then and took the wonderful smell with her.

This last time, though, I was minding my own business and enjoying a rare moment of peace and quiet when I felt the pull. I was instantly standing at the construction zone. Behind the tarps, I could see a fancy hotel on fire. The one downtown that all the business travelers stay at. I could see it ablaze, and I could see kids asleep. They were in trouble. Real trouble. I thought hard about Sam. I woke him up. He needed to help the kids. And he did. I don't remember much after that, but I knew that he had helped them. I knew it was okay. I could breathe a sigh of relief then. I went back to my relaxing.

38

Inside the brightly colored southern café, Hannah and Sam wash down gourmet pork chops and collard greens with sweet tea. Sam swallows a huge piece of cornbread slathered in butter.

Hannah gives him a gross-out look.

Sam shrugs. "What can I say? For some reason, I'm craving cornbread."

Hannah smiles at him and signs something like *letter* and *recipe*.

Sam just gives her a look and changes the subject. "So, what's the deal with Travis?"

Hannah reads his lips and blushes.

Sam wipes his mouth and signs, "I like him."

Hannah replies in her special cadence, having practiced controlling her volume over the years so as not to yell in public. "He's"—she signs as she speaks—"an illustrator. Comic books."

"The creative type. I get it." Sam smiles and butters another corn muffin.

"You know us artists. We—" Hannah makes two circles with both thumbs and index fingers and pulls them apart, then makes two fists and brings them together.

117

Sam smiles. "Stick together. Right . . . Is that what you were doing last night on the back porch?"

Hannah blushes a little, and they both laugh out loud.

A woman returning to her table notices them and stops. "Hannah?"

Hannah hops up in response and hugs the woman. Kate Beck smiles at Sam over Hannah's shoulder.

"Kate! What are you doin' downtown? I didn't think you could get Jack off the lake," Sam muses.

Kate points to a full table in the corner. Conrad Jr., Ariel, Paulo, and the other Banes—Candy, Jeffrey, Michelle, and little Wilson—feast on iced tea and fried chicken. Jack, at the head of the table, scarfs down a mound of onion rings and waves to Sam.

"He leaves the lake only if fried food is involved," Kate replies with a warm look at her husband.

Hannah grabs Kate's hand and examines a three-stone diamond ring. "Nice rock."

Kate heavily enunciates her words for Hannah. "Anniversary gift from Jack."

Sam inspects the white-gold setting. "Glad to hear he's finally appreciating you. Although I'll have to rethink his bonus. That's a paperweight, for God's sake."

"What's going on here?" a voice calls from the aisle between tables.

Sam looks up, stunned, to see Sara Parker approach their table. Before Sam can get a word out, Sara, Hannah, and Kate squeal in a group hug. Sara smiles at Sam over Hannah's shoulder. Against his will and better judgment, he cracks a smile.

39

Alex

Today, if it's a day at all—I'm really not sure—I have no will to live. Or be dead. I feel like an anchor at the bottom of a lake full of honey or molasses. I can't move or go to the construction zone or see anyone, even Big Gray and his friends. Everything that's usually white is gray and misty and cold. I wish I could sleep. A while ago, before this cold mist set in, Big Gray brought a lady to stand by me in the construction zone. She was young and pretty and dressed in a vintage stewardess uniform with silver wings pinned to her chest. She had a great smile, and when she touched my arm, I felt a really strong surge. But this feeling was nothing like the happy feeling from the Civil War guy. This feeling was urgent and pressing and prickly. It made me feel like I needed to run.

When I tried to move away from her, the flight attendant held tight to me like her life depended on it. Which is ironic, I know. Anyway, I looked through the tarps. At first, they were hazy with dark forms moving behind them. They began to clear into a bedroom and a closet. In the mirrored doors of the closet, I saw something horrible. The stewardess was lying on the bed, her eyes wide open, frozen in fear. I looked at the lady standing next to me and looked back at her double lying on the bed. The only difference between them was that the woman on the bed was younger and had red hair instead of blonde. The blonde stewardess holding my arm nodded to me and without a word, I knew what I had to do. There was still time to help the redhead. I had to raise an alarm.

Sam and Sara survey an indoor pool from an observatory level. On the pool stairs, university researchers attach a bright yellow helmet and electrodes to a bald man's head.

"I'm glad you came, Sam," Sara says, eyes forward.

Sam loosens his tie and glances at her profile. "I was under the influence when I agreed to this last night."

Sara looks at him, eyebrows raised.

Sam grins. "Sweet tea."

Sara smiles and returns her gaze to the pool below. "You said you had another episode?"

Sam nods and fidgets with his tie. "The fire at the Queen City Hotel. I got a message about it."

Sara looks at him without a hint of judgment.

"From Alex. I think. All these fires are started in different ways, but I have a hunch they're all connected."

"From Alex?"

Sam sighs. "I know it sounds totally crazy. But every time this happens, it feels like . . . she's there. Somehow."

"What do the police think?"

"That I'm a crazy person. Or a suspect."

Sara nods. "I bet."

"They want a statement about how I knew so much about the fire. I have no idea what to say to them." Sam shrugs.

Sara nods toward the experiment below. "I think Dr. Patel can help."

Sam surveys the scene with skepticism. Wearing swim trunks, the bald man in the pool sways as he steps into the water.

"Dr. Patel is testing the effect of water on temporal lobe stimulation," Sara notes.

Sam furrows his brow, observing the spectacle through the glass.

"What's temporal lobe stimulation?"

"The research started with temporal lobe epilepsy patients, some of whom have reported religious experiences in addition to seizures."

"I've never heard of that."

"I'm not sure many of them wanted to go public. Some believe famous prophets, like Moses, may have had TLE."

In the pool, the bald man wobbles into the water, assisted by gloved assistants.

"A few years ago, researchers attempted to replicate those experiences by stimulating the temporal lobes of the brain artificially. To produce what they call a God Reaction."

Sam watches the bald man. He gnaws on his lower lip.

"Subjects experienced a feeling beyond themselves, sensing a presence even when they were alone—that type of thing."

"What have you gotten me into here, Sara?" Sam asks as a bead of sweat rolls down his cheek. He wipes it away.

"At least talk to Dr. Patel. He is one of the country's leading experts in this field. The university is heavily investing in his work," Sara replies, full of confidence in spite of the strange experiment happening below.

In the pool, the bald man loses his balance due to the weight of the helmet, then splashes into the pool. Sam watches as the researchers swarm around him.

Sam exhales loudly. "What's this Patel guy a doctor of anyway?"

ℭℵℰ

Inside Dr. Patel's lab, Sam reads a framed degree on the wall— INDRA PATEL, PHD, MD, PSYCHOLOGY, PARAPSYCHOLOGY, NEUROLOGY, NEUROTHEOLOGY.

He wriggles on an examination table. The lab door opens, and a kid glides into the room on sneaker-skates. About twenty, the young man sports spiky black hair and a vintage A-Team T-shirt that reads *I love it when a plan comes together.*

He rolls up to Sam and sticks out a hand. "Hey! I'm Dr. Patel. But my friends call me Indy." Indy pops a wad of grape bubble gum loudly.

Only then does Sam notice the stethoscope hanging around the young man's neck.

"You're Dr. Patel?" Sam asks, mouth agape.

"Sure am, Sam." Dr. Patel skates to his desk. "Hey, that rhymes! Cool." Indy unearths a computer from a pile of papers and boots it up.

Sara enters the lab, followed by Molly, a voluptuous female assistant sporting a large butterfly tattoo on her chest. "Great, I see you met Dr. Patel," Sara says to Sam.

Sam gives her a deadly stare, but she presses on. "Dr. Patel is an internationally published expert in neurotheology."

Molly places a bright yellow helmet on Sam's head and attaches electrodes to his temples. "You're in good hands, Mr. Abernethy," she breathes.

Sam smiles weakly into Molly's butterfly, which wiggles as she moves.

Dr. Patel skates back to Sam. "Neurotheology is a cutting-edge—no, *bleeding*-edge—field of brain science that explores the connection between the temporal lobes of the brain and religious experiences."

The color drains from Sam's face, and he peers around Molly's boobs. "Look, Dr. Patel, this is a mistake."

"Call me Indy."

Sara puts a calming hand on Sam's arm. His shirtsleeves are rolled up, and beads of sweat line his brow. "Sam, it's okay. Trust me here. Dr. Patel graduated high school at twelve years old, college at sixteen, and medical school last year. He's doing his residency in neurology and teaching parapsychology here at the university."

Indy grins. "Try finding time for a date with that schedule. Even if I had one, I couldn't buy her a drink. I don't turn twenty-one until next month."

Sam's eyes grow large. Sara squeezes his wrist and gives an affirming nod.

"Molly, can you grab me the tablet from the break room? There's some notes on there I need."

"Sure thing, Doctor." Molly pats Indy playfully on the rear before leaving the office.

Indy searches through papers on his desk. "Sara told me about the handwriting match. I've worked with clairvoy-ants, remote viewers, even matter manipulators, but never spontaneous writing. It's an evidential physical connection to those who have passed."

Indy hands a yellow legal pad and pen to Sam. "Concrete evidence of life after death. Radical."

"Dr. Patel thinks that if we stimulate your brain to create this 'God Reaction,' that pathway to the divine—or whatever it is—may be opened. We could get some insight into your episodes."

Sam thrusts the notepad back into Indy's hands and begins fiddling with his helmet. With escalating panic, he says, "I came here to *stop* this from happening. I don't want to stimulate anything!"

Indy pushes the notepad back into Sam's hands. "Have you experienced any physical sensations, nausea, dizziness? Because sometimes the body can't handle that type of spiritual energy and—"

Sam throws the notepad to the ground and yells, "Enough!" He pants in choppy exhales, clutching his throat with one hand, short of breath.

Indy nods. He takes a deep break and pulls up a stool. He closes his eyes, inhales deeply, and exhales a long *ommmmm*. When Indy opens his eyes, he seems to emit a wisdom beyond his years. "Sam, I understand you and your sister were very close."

"We were," Sam whispers. Tears form in his eyes.

"I've seen stuff you wouldn't believe, man." Indy smiles calmly and warmly. Eventually Sam meets his eyes. "I've seen evidence that those connections—*especially* in siblings—can produce amazing results: mind reading, shared feelings, and extrasensory communication."

"But what does this have to do with me? With the episodes?" Sam asks, shaken.

"I believe it's possible for such an essential connection to linger after death," Indy says, with no hint of levity in his tone.

Sam stares at Indy and Sara. It takes every ounce of will he possesses to restrain the tears perched on his eyelids. He holds out his hand in silent consent. Indy returns the notepad to Sam.

"I'll wait outside," Sara says. She closes the lab door behind her.

"You ready?" Indy asks.

Sam nods his assent.

Indy presses a button on the computer, which whizzes to life. "The program will run by itself. It only takes a few minutes, and the nodes on the helmet will pick up the data we need. I don't want to be a distraction to you, so I'll leave you for a few minutes. Okay?"

"Okay."

Indy joins Sara in the hallway, and they head toward the breakroom.

In Dr. Patel's office, Sam sits alone, watching the computer monitor. The program initiates, and after a minute or two, Sam finally relaxes. A soft buzz indicates the magnets have been activated. Sam feels nothing.

He looks around the room. His nose itches. He waits. A few long minutes pass, and then he feels a strange sensation in his head, like he's swimming underwater. It doesn't feel right. It's like a tunnel closing in on him. Suddenly the feeling lifts. He sees every particle in the room spin like planets. A sense of peace and calm envelops him like a heated blanket. He watches as the computer melts onto the floor.

Next, the desk, the file cabinets, the door, even walls melt away, exposing a sunny yard.

At the school play, Sam is dressed as a tree. Alex swings in on a vine and yodels like the king of the jungle. A mountain bike rolls to a stop after a wicked jump on a dirt track. Alex pulls off her helmet and waves to Sam, who studies on the sidelines. Alex stands half out of the sunroof of a speeding sportscar and throws her graduation cap into the air. Sam pulls her down. A leather-jacketed bad boy rolls to a stop on a motorcycle. Alex jumps on the back and laughs. Sam watches them speed away. Alex, in a wedding gown, pulls off her garter and throws it to the crowd. Her bad-boy husband carries her to the limo. At a shabby home, Sam picks up Alex, who carries a suitcase and a crying baby Hannah. Alex waves goodbye from the number three stock car at the speedway. A bright white light envelops her.

Sam sits in the darkened lab. The computer program has ended, and the walls are back in place. Sam yanks the helmet from his head, leans forward, and pukes violently into a trash can.

Alex's spirit, watching from the corner, gags in sympathy.

Sam rights himself and grasps the pen tightly. He scribbles across the yellow legal pad in a fury of words.

A few minutes later, Sara holds a cold cloth to Sam's head. Indy wipes a spot of vomit from the yellow legal pad. The young genius reads the top page quickly, tears it off, and hands it to Sam. "I think we should deliver this one personally."

41

Inside the police department, Detective Kelly stares at Sam and Sara. The burly detective yells out the open office door, "Jimmy, get in here!"

Sara taps the page of yellow legal paper on the desk. "Detective, doesn't what we told you mean anything to you?"

"What have you told me? That this nutcase"—he points to Sam—"is some secretary for dead people? And this"—he holds up the yellow sheet of paper—"will predict the next victim of our boy here?"

Detective Kelly gestures to a poster hanging on the wall. It bears a sketch-artist rendition of a surly man with a large scar over one eye. The photo caption reads *Wanted for serial rape and murder. Report information about this man to the Charlotte Police Department.*

"If you just read the note, Detective," Sara pleads.

Detective Kelly scans the letter. It's addressed to Carol Graham at 4210 Washington Road. "Carol, dear, it's Grandma Graham. I don't know if this will reach you in time, but I must warn you, or someone that can help you. There is a bad man on the news. He has a scar over one eye, and he's hurt others. Please go to the police this Thursday, two p.m. sharp. Tell them to check your house."

Sam checks his watch. "It's one thirty."

The detective breathes deeply. "And what exactly are you expecting? I've half a mind to book you for the Queen City Hotel fire, Abernethy."

"I'll tell you everything I know about that. But first, please help us. We're running out of time," Sam begs.

Jimmy, the young officer from the hotel fire, enters the office. Sam and Jimmy exchange a nod of recognition.

Detective Kelly shows Jimmy the letter. "Is there a Carol Graham in the serial's file?"

Jimmy's eyes dart to the wanted poster. He shakes his head no.

"We already told you, my doctor thinks this could be a warning," Sam says. "He hasn't attacked her yet." His face reddens in frustration.

Detective Kelly peers through the open door at Indy, who does a handstand against a pretty female officer's desk. He harrumphs, "Some doctor."

Jimmy says, "I know that file inside and out. I can tell you no one by the name of Graham shows up in this guy's file."

"Carol Graham is not a victim . . . yet. That's the whole point of the letter," Sara says, exasperated.

"Forget it, Sara. We'll just find her ourselves." Sam stands, knocking the chair backward.

The old desk chair creaks as Detective Kelly groans and stands. "Hold on, you two." He hands the letter to Jimmy.

"Jimmy, send some black-and-whites to this address." He nods at Sam and Sara. "And take these lunatics with you."

✑✧

Across the street from a small bungalow with blooming flower boxes under each window, Sam and Sara watch as Jimmy and two uniformed officers approach Carol Graham's red front door.

Jimmy knocks and waits. Eerily, the door glides open, apparently unlocked. Jimmy nods silently to the officers. They sweep inside.

Inside the house, Jimmy and the officers tiptoe quietly down the hallway. A bedroom door is open. Jimmy looks inside. Carol appears to be sleeping on her side, facing the closet. In the doorway, Jimmy signals the officers and nods toward the sliding mirrored closet doors. The officers creep inside as Carol's eyes pop open and stare at the closet in terror.

Next instant, the closet doors explode into shards as a disheveled man bearing a prominent scar over one eye crashes onto the bedroom floor. The officers are knocked to the ground, but Jimmy is ready. He strikes the rising man. The butt of his gun connects with the man's forehead, sending blood splattering.

✑✧

Outside the bungalow, Jimmy and the officers walk the handcuffed man toward the police car and roughly push him inside. Sam and Sara watch the scene, thunderstruck.

42

Alex

I followed Sam today. He took the message from the pretty flight attendant to the police. I don't think they believed him. I do know that whatever that crazy doctor did to him pulled me past the tarps and into the world, into the room even, with my brother. It was the happiest feeling in the world to me. I loved it. He was upset by all of it, and I could sense that he is still trying to work out what happened to me. I wish I could remember more about that.

It was a real joy to see Sara too. I wished we'd stayed friends after she and Sam broke up. But life doesn't work that way, does it? I think she's good for him, though. She's like me—a total badass with a great actual ass.

Let's hope he doesn't screw it up. Again.

43

Hannah peers outside the window and takes in the view. A small cove, private and lush, opens up to a broad view of Lake Norman. On the yard leading up to the dock, Hannah spots a cardinal perched on a nearby oak branch. Its black-capped head moves jerkily from side to side, and its beak opens in a silent call. Hannah laughs to herself, thinking, *Fly away while you can!* Hannah is pulled back into the room as Kate and Sara pull together the back of a puffy pink gown and zip it up.

"I look like a cupcake," Hannah says, rounding the consonants in her unique style of speaking. She looks at her reflection in the full-length mirror attached to the room's closet. Her hands fly into the signs for *pink*, *cheesy*, and *cake*.

"It's amazing," Kate says to Sara, "how much brighter she looks out of all that dark stuff."

"Hey . . . I like my dark stuff," Hannah retorts.

Sara adjusts a puffy pink sleeve. "I'd say you are perfectly on theme for an Awesome 80's prom."

"And perfectly pretty in pink." Kate winks at Hannah in the mirror.

Hannah rolls her eyes and grins. It's clear that even she approves of the dress and loose updo of her purple-streaked silver hair dotted with tiny white flowers pinned into her wavy locks.

"Meet us outside near the deck, and we'll get some great photos," Kate says, clapping her hands together like the mother of the bride.

Sara checks her phone and taps Hannah on the shoulder. "Sam and Travis are a few minutes away."

Hannah's cheeks redden a little. She smiles and floats out of the room. Looking outside the window, Sara can see Hannah make her way to the dock, where Jack is sitting on a chair. Upon seeing her, Jack jumps up and bows deeply. Hannah curtsies.

Inside the bedroom, Kate and Sara collect the trappings of the makeover session: hair glitter, a curling iron, a makeup caddy, bobby pins, and tiny white paper flowers.

"So, Alice is the woman's mother?" Kate asks.

Sara shakes her head no. "Grandmother. She passed six months ago."

"What do the police say about Sam's letter?" Kate presses.

"The detectives are skeptical—even after I matched the handwriting to writing samples from letters Alice sent to her granddaughter, Carol." Sara stuffs Hannah's jeans and black hoodie into a fatigued duffel bag covered with pins and dots of multicolored paint.

"That's unbelievable," Kate replies, hoisting Hannah's backpack over her shoulder.

"Her grandmother saved her with that letter," Sara says, heading for the bedroom door.

"But Sam wrote the letter, right?" Kate asks, following.

"Well, his body did." Sara shuts off the lights in the spare bedroom.

"Do you believe in all that stuff?" Kate says, exiting into the living room with Sara.

Sara shrugs. "I believe in Sam."

☙

On the dock, Jack and Hannah shoot a few selfies. Sam and Travis walk toward them on a stone path leading from the driveway to the dock. Hannah waves at Travis, spiffed up in a gray suit with coordinating pink handkerchief. He carries a single pink-and-white rose. Hannah smiles and accepts the rose with a kiss on the cheek for Travis.

Sara and Kate join the group. "Okay, photo time!" Kate booms. "Sam, you and Hannah first. . . . Then we'll get the happy couple, and then a group shot, of course. . . . And I'd like to get the sunset too. . . ."

Travis taps on an imaginary watch. "We only have four hours until the prom, so . . ."

"Ha-ha," Kate says, exaggerating. She begins snapping.

Twenty minutes and a hundred pics later, Sam holds up a hand and turns to Kate. "Ma'am, put your weapon on the ground."

Kate pretends to be appalled and finally ceases the snapping. Jack takes her in his arms and dips her wildly, planting a sloppy kiss that misses her mouth.

"I'm going to walk the kids out to meet their ride," Sam says, holding up his phone. "Be right back."

Sam and Hannah walk ahead. Travis starts to follow, but Sara takes his arm and whispers, "Give them a minute." Travis and Sara slow their walk and remain a little bit behind uncle and niece.

Alone for a moment at the driveway circled by pines, Hannah peers at Sam. Her eyes, he can see, are a little watery. Sam grabs a tissue from his pocket and hands it to Hannah. She stuffs it into her tiny, beaded handbag.

Sam turns Hannah's face to meet his gaze and enunciates so she can read his lips. "You look beautiful. Your mother would be proud of you." Sam crosses his hands over the middle of his chest—the sign for *love*.

Hannah signs to him, unable to speak.

He nods. "I wish she were here too." He hugs his niece tightly before letting her go.

A moment later, a black sedan pulls into the driveway, and Travis joins his date. The young couple climbs into the car and waves on the way out, then turns their attention only to each other.

Sara approaches Sam as he watches them drive away. She holds his arm to steady him. "You did great."

Sam takes a deep breath and holds in the tears as long as he can.

44

Sam and Sara enter Sam's darkened living room.

"Thanks for tonight, Sara. It meant a lot to Hannah that you were there," he says, very close to her face, which is unclear in the darkness.

Sara jingles her car keys inadvertently. "No problem. It was good to see her happy again." She fidgets in the open doorway and says, "Well, I'm gonna get going."

Sam studies the floor. She turns to leave, but Sam speaks, almost a whisper. "I couldn't, you understand."

"Couldn't what?" Sara flips on a small table lamp in the entryway and looks more closely at Sam.

Sam's face is a picture of strain. His eyes are glued to the dark wood floor of the hallway. He clenches his teeth, and his words come out stilted. "Couldn't allow myself any happiness. I couldn't reach out. Not when Alex was—"

Sara's heart can almost be heard beating in the silence of the space between them. "I know. I wouldn't have expected you to—worry about me."

Sam expels a guttural wail and throws the small lit lamp violently to the floor. Despite the crash of ceramic, it remains intact and working. Its shaft of light spreads across Sam's shoes. He laughs quietly at his inability even to destroy a lamp. Sam's eyes water, and he finally looks into Sara's eyes directly. She goes to him.

45

"**I** am pleased to bestow this honor to Conrad Bane Jr. for his bravery and heroism," Arnold Noble booms from the podium. He pins a medal to Conrad's suit jacket. "Conrad saved more than one life that night," says Arnold while nodding to Emily Weaver and her family, who are seated in the front row of the community center. The little girl smiles gratefully at Conrad and waves. He waves back. "And we are grateful for his selfless service as one of our city's great first responders."

A round of applause rises from the packed center. Someone in back yells "FDNY forever!" and Conrad raises an arm in solidarity. He shakes Arnold's hand and steps back into the line of firefighters being honored for the lives saved at the Queen City Hotel fire.

"You should be proud of your husband, Ariel," Paulo whispers to his cousin.

Ariel smiles at Paulo, who is seated next to her. "I am." She looks closer at Paulo's face. "You okay? *Pareces deprimido.*"

Paulo shakes his head no. "I'm not down. I'm just thinking of Consuela. We would have been married by now. She could be here in the audience wishing me well. Like you are for Connie."

"You should be up there too." Ariel pats her bulging belly. "You all should. The whole station."

Paulo shakes his head. "I didn't save a kid dangling from the sixth floor." He hesitates a moment and adds, "And I'm not a firefighter from New York."

Ariel rolls her eyes. "Give me a break. Does that really matter?"

"You'd be surprised. Pedigree goes a long way here in the South," Paulo says, straightening his tie. "And Latinos don't."

"Don't what?" Ariel asks, confused. "Go far?"

"It doesn't matter, Ariel," Paulo says. "I will play along. And one day, I'll get my chance to move up the ladder. I have plans. Lots of plans that will make Consuela proud of me. One day."

Ariel looks with concern at her cousin. "You look very tired, Paulo. You should get some rest. And come over for dinner later. I will make you my tamales. You love those."

Paulo smiles at his cousin, an uncharacteristically dark look on his face. "I do love your tamales." He pats her hand. "Another time."

46

Sam finishes a phone call as he enters the Charlotte Police Department's downtown precinct.

"I talked to Connie after the ceremony yesterday," Jack's voice echoes in Sam's phone. "From his contacts on the force, he says the police haven't come up with a motive on the fires yet."

Sam clicks the volume button down a notch to counteract his partner's naturally booming voice. "Go on."

"The fire marshal thinks it could be a professional, though. Firefighter or ex-cop. Someone who knows accelerants, placement of ignition devices—that kind of stuff. The setups were practically perfect for maximum effect."

Sam rubs his chin with his free hand. "I've been over the case file a million times," he says, deep in thought. "I was thinking ex-military with a war agenda. But the politicians, the Bergen brothers, are pro-military, and the protesters outside the Ahzartec Corporation are anti-war, anti-government. Maybe anti-Muslim radicals, or anti-Saudi groups?" Sam sighs.

"Have you found anything on that law firm that rented the sixth floor of the hotel?" Sam asks.

"Still digging," Jack replies.

Sam sighs heavily. "Nothing makes sense."

"Are you sure the fires are all connected? Fire marshal says each one was started differently."

Sam approaches the glass doors of the police department. "Hey, I'm here, Jack. Let me see what I can find out from Detective Kelly. Call you back."

"Ten-four, partner."

ɷ

Sam wends his way through the busy police precinct. As he approaches Detective Kelly's office, Sam is shocked to see Sara at his desk. Instinctively, Sam moves to rescue her, but Jimmy deposits him in a chair outside.

"You'll get your chance," Jimmy says, the freckles on his pale skin glowing a little in anticipation of possible resistance.

Sam is seated in a small plastic chair big enough for a second grader. "What's going on, Jimmy? Sara has nothing to do with all this."

Jimmy doesn't respond. Both men peer inside Detective Kelly's glass office and see Sara hand a letter to him. The detective's brow crinkles in confusion as he reads.

Jimmy snorts. "Doesn't look that way to me."

47

Sam digs through the mess on his scratched mahogany coffee table. He rifles through old bills, hair ties, stiff paint brushes, trash, and unwashed glasses. Sara paces in front of the picture window overlooking the oak-laden front lawn. Bright sun streams through green leaves quilting the yard in lacey shadows.

"I had no choice but to show him copies of the paper-towel and crayon letters, Sam," Sara says, chewing on a thumbnail. "They pulled me in for questioning and told me they found the cigarettes and paint thinner, just like you said. They told me they're putting you on the list as an arson suspect!"

"Yeah, but they don't have enough yet," Sam says, pushing aside a stack of mail. "Unless you gave them enough."

Sara's knees give out a little, and her shoulders sag with frustration and worry. "I thought the other letters, along with the match I did for Alice Graham, might prove that your information is coming from—"

"From where?" Sam snaps. He wiggles his fingers. "Beyond the grave? Thanks a million, Sara. They already think I'm a flake." Sam tosses a pizza box to the floor.

"Why?" Sara urges. "Because you saved a young woman from being raped and killed? And those kids at the hotel could be dead if you hadn't called for help when you did!" Sara speaks rapidly. "I gave an expert opinion as to the origin of the letters you've been writing. If we prove they're not in your handwriting, and I can match them to a real source, maybe the police will believe you are not involved in any of this."

"But I am involved," Sam says. "Ah-ha!" he exclaims suddenly. Sam inspects two small silver charms and stuffs them in his pocket. "Just please stay out of it. I don't want you hurt because of me."

Sara nods and seals her mouth into a hard line. She is so angry she literally cannot speak. She slams the front door behind her.

Sam stares at the door for a second, pondering this. He grabs a half-full bottle of whiskey from the table and downs a huge slug.

☙

In the driveway, Sam stops Sara at her car, a practical silver sedan. He turns her toward him.

Sara's eyes begin to fill with tears. "Not everything, including your sister's death, is your responsibility, Sam."

"Sara, I'm sorry." Sam starts toward his black SUV parked on the road. "I gotta go see about something. I'll call you later?"

Sara sighs. "Okay . . . but where are you—"

Sam enters his vehicle in a flash and speeds off.

Sara deflates.

48

Jimmy knocks on the front door of a colonial ranch house. Next to the door, a gleaming brass plate is engraved with the occupants' name and address: The Masons, 34405 W. Fahrenheit Way.

Jimmy rings the bell and waits. He straightens his gun belt. After a minute, Judge Mason, dressed for golf, opens the heavy wooden door. The slightest wave of panic crosses his face as he notices the unmarked police car parked along the road behind Jimmy. Another officer can be seen in the car, punching in something on the car's dash-mounted computer.

"Good afternoon, Judge Mason. Can I have a word, sir?"

"About what?" The judge wipes one bead of sweat from his cornrow-like hairline of silver implanted follicles.

Jimmy holds up an envelope that has been torn open, as well as a letter scrawled in childlike red crayon. "About this."

49

Sam approaches Madame Amanda's tiny purple house. He knocks. Madame Amanda opens the door and smiles widely. She beckons him inside with a hand on her pregnant belly. "Well, I'll be! Never thought I'd see you again."

Sam closes the door behind him. "I don't want another eye reading."

Amanda chuckles. "I won't hurt ya. Promise." She plops into one of two matching brown recliners in her small living room and breathes deeply. Somehow soothed by this, Sam takes the other chair.

The television is muted, but Sam sees reality-show housewives getting pedicures in a posh salon. Lincoln is sound asleep on a blanket.

He turns to Amanda. "It's happened again."

Amanda rocks a few times and nods. "Thought it might."

Sam pulls the silver charms from his pocket. "This has something to do with it. I don't know what."

Amanda takes the silver eagle and owl charms and rolls them around in her palms. "There's some energy here, but it's unclear."

"These were at two of the arson sites. My partner, Jack, found the eagle at the Ahzartec explosion . . ." Sam trails off at the memory.

"Where Alex was killed?" Amanda asks.

Sam nods. "And I found the owl at the site of the Bergen political office that was torched. I also saw a falcon, same size, that the police found at the Queen City Hotel fire. They must be important. I was wondering if you could . . . like . . .I don't know. I don't understand this stuff. Alex was the spiritual one, or whatever. Could you read them?"

Amanda takes a deep breath and holds the charms in her palms for a minute.

Sam stares through the hallway into the reading room. The wooden mask on the far wall stares at him with white-rimmed, vacant eyes.

"Your connection to your sister is quite strong," Amanda says. "And these are connected to her somehow. Like a message for you. I am not sure exactly."

"Anything else?" Sam says with urgency.

"I'm sorry, Sam. That's all I can tell you, honey. You're on the right track, I think." Amanda hands the charms back to Sam.

"Okay, thanks," Sam says, a little disappointed. He studies the floor.

"What else is on your mind, Sam? You are trying to figure all this out with the letters and such—I understand that. Can you tell whether any of them are connected to your sister?"

"They are about people and places I don't know, have no connection to. I don't know that Alex had any connection to them either. They have nothing to do with me."

Amanda sighs. "Well . . . maybe they have to do with her. With Alex. Where she is now."

"You think they're related to her death?" Sam asks. "Like clues?"

Amanda shrugs and rocks a minute. "I don't see that."

Sam bites his lip. "This is so goddamn frustrating! I have no idea what to do—how to stop this and get back to my life. I don't understand why—I don't give a rat's ass about these people or helping anyone, actually. I just don't understand what's happening, and I'm going to lose it if I don't get some answers."

Amanda gets up from the chair, waddles to Sam, and kneels before him. She takes his hands in hers and says, "Breathe, Sam."

He does as she asks.

"Tell me what's really bothering you about all this? It ain't the letters, or the people, or the tiny birds. What is it?"

Sam stares into Amanda's light-blue eyes. Something in them allows him to speak the truth. Finally, he whispers, "I miss her. Every day. Every minute."

Amanda nods.

"And I don't understand where she is and why—with all the messages for everyone else—why hasn't she talked to me? Why haven't I heard from her? I'm her brother. I don't care about any of the rest of this. If I have to go through it, fine, but when will I get a message—something for me, for Hannah? Can you tell me that?"

Amanda's eyes are filled with tears now. She smiles and pats Sam on the hand before struggling to rise. Sam helps her.

"That's the truth, Sam. You said the truth." Amanda walks toward the door. "I don't have the answer, but sometimes, the only place to start is with the question."

Sam and Amanda walk onto the front porch. The sun is shining brightly and warms their faces. Amanda rubs her big belly. Sam reaches his car and opens it. He turns back.

"My granny once told me the secret to life," Amanda calls out. "It's something that I often think 'bout when times are troublin'."

"Oh yeah, what's the secret?" Sam says.

"Bacon grease," Amanda replies and lifts a small hand in goodbye.

Sam shakes his head. "Makes sense."

"But then again, Granny got all her information from the *National Enquirer.* She called it her 'Bible,' so you can take it with a grain of salt."

Sam waves, closes the car door, and drives away.

☙

Inside the purple house, Amanda plops onto the couch. Her back is killing her. She thinks about Sam and Alex. Two people could not be more different. She ponders this and exhales deeply as Lincoln, rubbing sleep from his eyes, waddles over to her. Amanda looks down at the toddler.

"Who you?" Lincoln asks.

"What you mean, baby?" Amanda says. "It's Momma."

Lincoln shakes his head no.

Amanda is taken aback for a second but realizes instantly she's not speaking. Another voice is coming from her mouth. A voice she recognizes. It's warm and has no accent. Amanda drifts behind her own mind. Alex, using Amanda's hand, tussles Lincoln's hair and says, "You are getting so big! You must be a handful to your mom."

Lincoln laughs at this with his high-pitched little giggle. He stuffs his pacifier back into his mouth and waddles away.

From somewhere behind Alex's voice in the recesses of Amanda's mind, she says *hey* to Alex and asks Alex to pick up the hand mirror on the coffee table. Alex does so.

They look into the reflection, which is Amanda, but also Alex. Amanda's blue eyes are now brown, and her perky nose is longer. When she smiles, Amanda's grin presents a dimple on the left side which doesn't belong to her but is reminiscent of Alex's cute grin. The effect lasts only a moment. Within seconds, the transformation is over, and Amanda is back. The reflection is all hers again.

Amanda wonders if it was real. She always heard the voices and saw visuals of things. Things people never told her. But she never shared herself with anyone before. Not like this. She feels a little sick, like she's going to throw up. She takes a few deep breaths and calls for Lincoln. Her voice is hoarse, but it's hers again. Lincoln runs to greet his mama.

50

Alex

Big Gray started hanging out with me pretty much all the time. He's a pest, but at least his friends aren't around anymore. He wants me to tell him everything I'm seeing when I'm at the construction zone. About the city and the fires. He's real interested in what Sam's doing and the investigation that's going on with the fires at Ahzartec (the cause of my demise), this political guy's office, and the hotel. He runs his giant hands through that crazy gray mane of his, and he keeps jawing about someone named Candy. Or Connie. I can't tell which.

Speaking of hair, I had a very weird experience recently. Big Gray was off somewhere, leaving me a moment to myself. Through the tarps, I saw Sam meeting with an old friend of mine. She was my hairdresser and psychic. Great combination. I could get highlights and a reading all in one afternoon. I loved her, and she helped me through many tough times. I really wanted to hear what they were talking about. So, I focused all my energy on Madame Amanda. I thought about her and her purple house and her warm smile. I stepped toward the tarps, and I pushed them aside. I had never touched them before. Never thought to. When I did, Amanda's radiant energy surrounded me, and I was sort of pulled into her. For just a second. In that moment, I was stretched thin, like a rubber person with half of me here and half of me there. It only lasted a few seconds. I just missed Sam, who had left a few minutes back.

I know my brother is suffering. I was hoping I could talk to him somehow. And I think if I tell him about Big Gray and the birds, it may help. I don't know why I think so, but I want to tell him he's on the right track.

Hannah and Sam lunch on the terrace of their favorite pizza joint. The sun shines brightly on their iced teas, transforming the glasses into light-brown kaleidoscopes.

Hannah gobbles down a breadstick in two bites and wipes her mouth. "You don't have to keep checking on me." She signs, "I'm fine."

Sam signs, "I know. Can't I have lunch with my niece on a Saturday once in a while?"

Hannah smiles and nods.

Breaking the moment, Jack approaches the terrace.

"Hey, you two!" Jack bellows. "Am I too late for pizza?"

"Right on time," Hannah says and hands him a slice of four-cheese pizza.

Jack pulls up a chair and stuffs the slice into his mouth in one movement. He drops a folder in front of Sam, who opens it and skims through articles featuring the Twin Towers.

"Check this out. I found Collique & Partners," Jack mumbles with a mouth full of crust. He swallows hard and raises a finger to a passing waitress. He mimics drinking and burping, pounding a closed fist on his chest.

The waitress chuckles. "The usual?"

Jack gives her a thumbs-up.

"And . . ." Sam says, leafing through the articles.

"The firm defended the city of New York in a suit filed by 9/11 families. They claimed the city ignored warnings that the fire department's handheld radios didn't work in the World Trade Center."

Sam furrows his brow.

The waitress sets a foamy beer in front of Jack, who nods in thanks.

Sam asks, "What else?"

Jack takes a long swig of beer. "They also defended several international banks named as terrorist supporters in the hundred-*trillion*-dollar 9/11 lawsuit back in '02. No one's returning calls about why they rented out the sixth floor of the Queen City Hotel and why they never showed." Jack shrugs.

Sam closes the file. "What are you doing downtown today anyway? I know how you live for the lake on the weekends."

Jack nods. "True, but I'm picking up a new suit for the fundraiser at the Raptor Institute tonight. Unfortunately, Ole Blue doesn't meet me in the middle anymore." He pats his beer belly.

Sam chuckles. "Good. Ole Blue belongs back in the nineties, from whence he sprang."

"What? Ole Blue was the perfect amount of baggy."

"For Chandler, Ross, and Joey, yes." Sam signs the credit card receipt. "Why don't you ride with me first? I'm dropping Hannah off at school for the afternoon—she's working on some art for a school exhibit. Then we'll visit the friendly hotel manager and see if he has any idea what Collique's plans were while they were here."

Jack nods and scoops up another slice.

Hannah taps Sam on the shoulder and points to her watch.

Sam nods to Jack. "Wolf it."

Jack obliges.

ↀ

Sam pulls up in front of the converted stone church that now serves as the Charlotte School for the Deaf. Hannah hops out of the car. Campus is empty, but a few students in paint-spotted coveralls eat brown bag lunches on the old stone wall that fronts the school. They wave at Hannah as she exits the car.

Sam turns to Jack. "It'll just take a minute. Hannah wants to show me the art studio. She's got a piece in an upcoming show."

"Cool." Jack smiles. "Our little Picasso."

Inside the studio, a high-ceilinged, light-flooded cavern of a room, Hannah points to her painting. A bright-pink bald eagle stares back at them. Sam smiles as if he's never seen one before. Jack gives Hannah a thumbs-up.

The next instant, Sam doubles over and catches himself on an empty desk, but his hand melts through the desk like taffy. He falls to the floor and ralphs.

Hannah hops backward away from the flow. Sam wipes his mouth on a sleeve and moves without hesitation to the dry-erase board. He grabs a marker and scrawls, then collapses to the floor.

"Sam! Are you okay?" Jack rushes toward Sam. He bends down and lightly slaps Sam's face. Jack helps him sit up.

Hannah hands her uncle a paper towel, and Sam wipes the corners of his mouth. He is sweating but seems to be coming back to himself. Sam, Jack, and Hannah stare wide-eyed at a message scrawled neatly on the board:

My brother and I once got lost in the woods. Turns out we were only a hundred yards from home. And so are you. Keep digging. You are on the right track. Talk to PV.

Hannah signs, "Who is PV?"

Sam and Jack exchange a knowing look. Jack snaps a picture of the dry-erase board on his phone.

Sam stares at the message on the board. He recalls the shaving cream message. That message didn't appear to come from someone else either. It was a direct warning or clue. Just like this. Could they both be messages from Alex? Were they clues to what happened to her? He thinks about Madame Amanda. Maybe he is on the right track, after all.

Hannah taps Sam on the arm, waking him from his trance.

Sam signs, "Explain later. Pick you up at three?"

Hannah nods.

Near the window, Alex's spirit self sits with her feet up on a student's desk and pretends to smoke. She nods, satisfied, as Sam and Jack make a quick exit. Alex then turns her attention to Hannah. She sends as much sunshine to her beautiful daughter as she can muster.

A golden shaft of light breaks through the clouds, illuminating Hannah and her bright-pink bald eagle. Hannah smiles and turns toward the source of the light—a large window situated over an empty desk. She squints. A light wisp of smoke curls toward the ceiling and disappears.

52

Ariel, pregnant and about to burst, waddles into her living room. Sam and Jack sit on the plastic-covered gold couch.

"Paulo should be back shortly. Can I offer either of you a beer?" Ariel says in dreamy, accented English.

Jack gives her a thumbs-up, but Sam cuts him off. "No, thanks—we're in a hurry."

Disappointed, Jack adds, "How about some of your amazing homemade chips?"

"Only for you, Jack." Ariel smiles and holds her back as she waddles into the kitchen.

Jack whispers to Sam, "I don't know why we're here, man."

"The message said to talk to PV—Paulo Vargas," Sam answers.

Jack calls to Ariel through the small living room into the kitchen. "You excited about tonight, Ariel?"

Ariel peeks her head around the corner and smiles. "Yes. I love the eighties cover band that's playing. They play all the best new wave. I'm going to crimp my hair in honor of the best decade ever."

The loud screech of a bird of prey emanates from the narrow hallway. Jack and Sam look toward the sound. Ariel's heavy sigh precedes her return to the living room. She carries a bowl of fresh tortilla chips on a tray, along with a bowl of fresh guacamole with cilantro.

"Just a moment, guys." Ariel sets down the tray and waddles along the hallway toward the screeching. She grabs a basket of prescription medication from a hallway table. "Coming, Mrs. Bane."

Sam and Jack exchange a knowing look when they understand the source of the screeching—Candy Bane, living in Conrad and Ariel's only spare bedroom.

"Hurry up, I'm in some pain here." Candy's raspy, high screech echoes through the narrow hall, and Sam is reminded of a baby pterodactyl.

"Where will the baby live when he or she gets here?" Jack says with a grimace. "In the garage?" He grabs a fresh tortilla chip and drags it across the bowl of fresh guacamole.

A few minutes later, Ariel returns carrying an emptied food tray. "Okay," Ariel says brightly upon her return. "She gets very antsy when it's time for her meds." She sets the messy tray on the kitchen counter and takes a seat across from Sam and Jack.

Reclining on the sofa, Jack asks, "Will we see you in the birdcage tonight?"

Ariel chuckles at the description of the mile-high glass atrium. "Yep." She kicks her feet up on a small stool. "I'm really excited to dress up for a change." She looks down at her big belly. "Even with the extra passenger."

Jack dances a little in his seat. "Kate made me promise to behave—apparently I've caused many people pain and suffering in the past when I hit the dance floor."

Ariel chuckles. "Me too." She turns to Sam. "What about you, Sam?"

Sam shakes his head dismissively. He checks his watch. "Sorry, but when do you think Paulo will be home? It's pretty important we speak with him."

Ariel furrows her brow. "Is something wrong?"

"We don't know exactly, but I . . . well, I got a message to . . . it's going to sound weird, but—"

Sam freezes. As Ariel bends forward to grab a chip, something around her neck glitters on a silver chain. Sam recognizes it.

He points to her chest. "Where'd you get that?"

Ariel fingers a silver eagle charm. "Birthday gift from Paulo. Very sweet."

Sam's mind races as dots connect in unseen corners of his psyche. "Can I borrow that?" Sam says, rising abruptly from the couch.

Ariel shoots Sam a puzzled look. She shrugs. "Sure." She removes the chain and hands it to Sam.

"I'll get this right back to you. Thanks so much," Sam says and heads toward the front door.

"Boss?" Jack asks.

"You stay and have a chat with Paulo, okay? I'll come back as soon as I can," Sam adds hastily.

"Sure," Jack says with a crinkled brow. He stuffs another chip in his mouth and smiles at Ariel. "Now . . . about that beer . . . "

೧೪೦

Inside the North Carolina Raptor Institute Gift Shop, Sam lifts a prepackaged eagle charm from a wire rack. He holds it up next to Ariel's necklace.

He speaks into his phone. "It's a match. One of these bird charms was found at every arson site. We may be on to something."

On the phone, Jack replies, "I'm on the way home now. Paulo never showed up. Ariel said he was supposed to pick up his usher uniform from the dry cleaners over an hour ago. Listen to this. I chatted up Ariel after you ran out. It's about Consuela, Paulo's fiancée."

"Paulo told us she died in Colombia two years ago, before he came to the US," Sam replies.

"Yes," Jack continues. "But he didn't mention *how* she died. Consuela was killed in a university fire by a terrorist military faction of the government."

"Christ," Sam says into the phone.

"Bad memories can twist the mind," Jack replies.

A young clerk smiles sweetly at Sam, who spins the rack of charms. "Those are really popular," she says and smacks her gum. The clerk raises her arm and jingles her own charm bracelet.

"Thanks, I'll take the eagle and the falcon. And can you help me with something?" Sam says, pulling a charred owl charm from his shirt pocket. The charm he found at the Bergen fire is barely recognizable, but the clerk nods and spins the rack. She hands a shiny new owl charm to Sam.

Sam says into the phone, "Hold a sec." He hands the girl a credit card. "I'll take this too." She rings up the charms. Into the phone, he says, "Jack, are the Colombians connected to al-Qaeda?"

"Dunno," Jack says, "but the faction that killed Consuela has certainly assimilated al-Qaeda's worldview on mass terror: bombings, murder, kidnapping, hijacking—the whole enchilada."

"Sir?" says the girl, rapidly blinking at hearing the words *kidnapping* and *murder*.

Sam holds up a finger. His mind races. "Jack, I can see it."

"See what?" Jack asks.

Sam's mind blazes into a vision, unbidden. Paulo, in heavy black boots, stands outside the Ahzartec building and presses a button on a cell phone. The building explodes. Paulo places a silver eagle charm next to the entrance. He touches fingertips to his lips and touches the tattoo of Consuela on his arm, transferring the kiss to his lost love. Later, at Senator Bergen's office, Paulo stands in the smoking rubble of the office and gently places the owl charm near the door with a gloved hand. At the Queen City Hotel, Paulo removes his firefighter's mask and carefully places a silver falcon outside the lobby of the hotel as flames erupt behind him. As he walks away, he smiles at Consuela's ink image on his forearm.

"Sir?" the clerk says with a sense of urgency.

Sam growls under his breath, "Just a sec!" Into the phone, he says, "Jack, I need you to call Detective Kelly and—"

The girl's eyes widen at something behind him. Sam turns to see Jimmy holding up a pair of handcuffs by one finger. "No need to call the detective, Abernethy," Jimmy says. He removes the cell phone from Sam's hand and ends the call.

"Jimmy! I need to talk to you," Sam says, oblivious to his situation.

"Samuel Abernethy, you are under arrest for the kidnapping and murder of Cecilia Mason. You have the right to remain silent—"

"What?" Sam asks, looking around the room as if waiting for someone to point out the mistake.

"We can do this the easy way"—Jimmy points to two uniformed officers outside the gift-shop door—"or the hard way."

"I don't know any Cecilia Mason! What the hell are you talking about?" Sam yells as Jimmy wrangles Sam's arms behind his back.

Suddenly, the clerk calls out to Sam. "Wait!"

She hands him a small bag containing the purchased owl, falcon, and eagle charms—just before Jimmy clicks the cuffs closed.

Jimmy and the officers lead Sam out the door, reading him his rights.

The clerk waves vacantly and says, confused, "Thanks for visiting the North Carolina Raptor Institute today. . . ."

53

Jimmy talks to Sam through the bars of a holding cell. "Judge Mason told us how you taunted him with a threatening letter about his missing daughter, Cecilia."

"I threatened him?" Sam yells. "It was the other way around! He nearly broke down my door, crazy bastard."

"And the letter? It was on your stationery." Jimmy stares hard at Sam through the holding cell bars.

Sam runs a hand through sweaty brown hair. "It's hard to explain, Jimmy. It was my niece; she pulled the letter out of the trash can. . . . I've been having these episodes. . . . It's like something comes over me and these messages come out. I know it seems crazy, but this letter was not mine. Not from me, you know? I mean, technically I wrote it, but look at it! It's not even my handwriting."

Jimmy stares at Sam without reaction.

Sam presses his eyelids closed and takes a deep breath, resetting. "What about my phone call?" Sam asks, tapping his ear maniacally with a finger.

Jimmy remains cool. "First, Detective Kelly wants a word with you about the hotel fire. Then you'll get your call. Funny how you always seem to be in the wrong place at the wrong time, Abernethy."

Sam's eyes widen as he remembers something. He pulls the prepackaged falcon, eagle, and owl charms from his pocket and thrusts them through the bars. "Look at these. . . . Where's the falcon you found at the Queen City? It will match. I also found an owl charm at Bergen's headquarters, and my partner found an eagle at Ahzartec. They all came from the Raptor Institute. The gift shop."

Jimmy's interest is piqued. He takes the packaged charms and inspects them.

"Paulo Vargas moonlights there as a security guard," says Sam. "He might be a little crazy. His fiancée was killed by terrorists. Something's wrong here."

Jimmy inspects the falcon charm. Reluctantly, he hands Sam a few quarters. "Five minutes."

He unlocks the holding cell and releases Sam. Sam runs down the hallway to the pay phone and yells back over his shoulder, "I owe you one, Jimmy!"

∽

Sam fidgets as the phone rings through the old-school handset. Finally, Sara picks up.

"Hello?"

"Sara, no time. I'm at the police station. They took my cell, and I can't text Hannah. I need you to pick her up from school and watch her till I can get out of here."

"Sam, what's going on?" Sara says on the other end of the line.

Sam grips the phone like a lifeline. "They arrested me for the kidnapping of the little girl in the letter. The crazy judge who attacked me is her father."

"What? Do the police think you were involved now? Is this because of the letters I gave them? Oh my God, I'm sorry, Sam."

"It doesn't matter. Just keep an eye on Hannah till I can sort this out. And find Jack. Neither he nor Ted picked up. Tell Jack to get here quick. It's urgent. About Paulo. We went to see the Banes today—Paulo, Conrad Jr. and Ariel—something's wrong there, and Paulo may be unstable. Jack and I aren't sure what's happening yet, but I really need you to find him. And grab my briefcase from the house—it has my files on the arson cases. Jack can bring them to me. Just find him now. Please, Sara."

"Okay, I'll track him down."

"Thanks."

Sam hangs up and dials both Ted and Jack again. He leaves two more voicemails before Jimmy removes the handset from his grip, hangs up the phone, and escorts him back to the holding cell.

54

Paulo knocks on Ariel's front door. "Hey," Paulo pants as Ariel opens the door. "Sorry—the cleaners took forever. Here's your dress. I gotta run, I'm running late." He hands his cousin a puffy gold dress covered in thin plastic. His Raptor Institute usher uniform is draped over an arm.

"Thanks. I was starting to worry, Paulo." Ariel chews on her lower lip. "Is everything okay? We'll see you later at the event, then?"

"Yeah, all good. Just a few things I need to take care of before I go." Paulo checks the time on his phone. "Conrad picking you up?"

Ariel nods and shoots her eyes toward the back corner of the tiny yellow house. "Yes, we're *all* going tonight." She widens her eyes and flashes a sarcastic smile.

Paulo nods in understanding. He jogs toward his house next door but turns back. "Quick question." Paulo points back to his open garage. There's a pile of stuff in the corner, not mine. Did Conrad store some supplies in my garage?"

"I don't know. Is that extra stuff from work, maybe? They had that skunk at the station last month. Maybe they cleared out closets or something?" Ariel shrugs. "Do you want me to call him?"

Paulo shakes his head. "No, don't bother him. I'll catch up with him tonight."

"Oh, hey," she calls. "Save me a dance tonight?"

Paulo sighs and smiles. "Only for you, cousin." Paulo jogs back into his house. He calls back over his shoulder. "And tell your husband to get his shit out of my garage."

55

Sara pulls into the circular drop-off zone at Hannah's school. Hannah smiles and reads a text message on her cell phone, which is also equipped with relay services. Hannah looks up to see Sara wave at her from a silver sedan.

Hannah opens the door to the passenger seat and shifts Sam's briefcase to the back seat before plopping down. She faces Sara. "Is everything okay?"

Sara nods yes and enunciates, "Sam is in jail, but it's a mistake."

"I didn't get a message." Hannah's eyes water a little. She checks her phone.

Sara gently turns Hannah's face up to read her lips. "They took his cell phone, so he can't message you." Sara says. "It will be okay. He wants us to find Jack. He needs to warn Jack about someone named Paulo."

Hannah recognizes the name from earlier that day and nods. "P-V. Sam got a message to talk to—" Hannah quickly types a note in her phone and shows it to Sara: *Paulo Vargas.* "He wrote it on the smartboard in my studio." She pulls up a photo of the message on her phone and shows Sara.

My brother and I once got lost in the woods. Turns out we were only a hundred yards from home. And so are you. Keep digging. You are on the right track. Talk to PV.

Sara nods, thinking. "Do you know about these . . . messages?"

Hannah nods. "The eagle says it's my mother." Hannah buckles her seat belt, unperturbed. "She sends the messages."

Sara contemplates this a moment and lets it go for now. "We need to find Jack," she says and puts the car in gear. "I called Kate, but there's no answer."

Hannah quickly signs, "Jack and Kate?"

Sara nods.

"I know where to go." Hannah pulls up the map on her smart phone and shows Sara.

Sara understands and hits the gas.

56

Paulo, dressed in black dress pants and a maroon collared shirt emblazoned with the Raptor Institute logo—a hawk perched atop the letters RI—answers a knock on his front door.

He pauses and looks around the yard. No one else is around. He smiles awkwardly and invites his guest inside.

57

Sara and Hannah wait in a line of cars at the main entrance of the Raptor Institute's Uptown location. The multi-story glass atrium reflects deep orange and pink hues as the sun sinks behind neighboring skyscrapers. Valet parking attendants in red polo shirts jog briskly to manage drop-offs and move vehicles to the nearby lot. Partygoers in semiformal attire make their way into the building past a heavy rotating door and attendants taking tickets inside.

Hannah taps Sara on the shoulder. "I can find Jack and Kate. I know they're here because they tried to get Sam to bring me tonight."

Sara pulls forward a few feet. "Are you sure?"

Hannah nods. She points to the tall, blond young man behind the valet stand. Sara recognizes Travis instantly from his floppy bangs and a hearing aid that wraps around a pierced ear.

Hannah hops out of the car and approaches him. They sign quickly to each other, and Travis waves Sara to a small driveway out of the line of cars.

"You can keep the car running." Travis bends into Sara's open passenger-side window. "I'll take her in, and we'll find Jack. Be right back."

Sara hesitates a second but relents. She nods and the kids disappear into the crowd.

58

At the police station, Detective Kelly approaches Sam in the holding cell.

Sam jumps from the cot and grabs the cell bars. "Detective, did you check out Paulo's house yet? Look for accelerants, timers maybe, and—"

Detective Kelly holds up a weathered, tan hand. "Paulo's dead."

Sam slaps the gray metal cell bars with both palms. "What? How?"

"Jimmy and the boys found him in the house a few minutes ago on your tip," says Detective Kelly. "Overdose. He left a note. Preliminary results indicate a cocktail of alcohol and some kind of opioid."

Detective Kelly shows Sam a note in a sealed plastic evidence bag. Sam inspects the blocky writing: *I tried to make it right and get justice for Consuela. I don't regret making the terrorists pay. The hotel, the senator, they all deserved it. But I did not mean to hurt those kids in the hotel. The lawyers were supposed to be there. I'm sorry. Consuela deserved better.*

"Also found supplies in his garage," Detective Kelly says, scratching the top of his balding head. "Electronic timers, gas and kerosene, fire boots, car batteries. All supplies similar to those used in every one of the arson cases."

Sam squeezes the back of his neck and paces inside the cell. "What did Connie have to say?"

"Who?"

"Conrad Bane. He lives next door to Paulo and he's married to Paulo's cousin, Ariel," Sam snaps.

The detective shrugs. "Neighbors weren't home on either side. But the officers on the scene are still knocking on doors in the neighborhood."

"Are you sure Paulo wrote the note?" Sam asks. "He may have been a little"—Sam twirls his index finger in circles near his head to indicate "loopy"—"but he didn't seem like the type to kick his own bucket."

"Initial review on the note was inconclusive. Toxicology reports may shed more light when they come in. We're working it now." The detective turns and begins walking down the hall.

"Call Sara Parker," Sam shouts after him. "She can verify the handwriting against fire department employment records I have in the Ahzartec file at home."

"We're working the case, Abernethy," Detective Kelly says over his shoulder. "I was just giving you a courtesy update based on your tip. But I'm not convinced you're not knee-deep in shit across the board here, so worry about yourself first."

Sam presses his lips together and groans. "Something is very wrong here, detective! I knew Paulo was off and somehow connected to this. But suicide? It doesn't feel right."

The detective loosens his wilting tie and turns back to face Sam. "Or maybe Paulo is just guilty. Maybe he lost his shit when he realized his quest for vengeance resulted in risking the lives of innocent kids. The simplest explanation is usually right."

"Detective, please!" Sam calls out. "Send the note to Sara Parker. Her contact info is in my phone. Ask her to verify your results. She can do it quickly." Sam clutches the cell bars. "Please!"

The skin on the detective's neck starts to turn red. "Why should I do anything for you, Abernethy? You're already a suspect in the Mason case, and I've half a mind to book you for the Queen City Hotel fire as well until we know more about this." He holds up the suicide note in the plastic bag.

Sam pleads with the detective. "Fine. You can book me. But that shouldn't stop you from doing the right thing. Sara is the best analyst in the business. At least let her take a look."

Detective Kelly sighs heavily. He trudges down the hall and out of sight.

59

Inside the ten-story glass atrium, party guests marvel at a falcon perched high above their heads. A hawk dips and swoops above a thin layer of netting that separates the highfliers from the patrons below. A young busboy on clean-up duty scans the furniture and floor for bird droppings and wipes them up discretely upon discovery.

Travis and Hannah traverse a field of round bar-height tables wrapped in black fabric and decorated with silver-and-gold centerpieces. Cocktail napkins and empty plastic drinkware litter the unoccupied tables, while others are surrounded by chattering guests munching on tiny quiches and bacon-wrapped fig appetizers.

Travis signs to Hannah and splits off to search near the restrooms and back hallway. Hannah dodges a waitress with a full tray of champagne cocktails and heads toward a familiar face near a temporary stage that's been set up for the band.

As Hannah pushes her way through the crowd toward Kate, a ripped-jeans-clad roadie sets up a microphone on stage. Ten yards behind him, Hannah recognizes the broad windows of the bird hospital. Black shades have been drawn so that the injured birds are not disturbed by the lights of the party. Hannah wonders about the effect of the music on the poor birds. She hopes that maybe they've been moved to the Raptor Institute's other location—woodsy acres north of town that she'd visited during her summer camp days.

Hannah approaches Kate, who stands next to a pregnant, caramel-skinned beauty sporting crimped black hair and a soap opera–style gold party dress. Hannah also notices a skinny older woman sitting a couple of feet lower than Kate in a wheelchair. The lady's white hair has been curled into a helmet, and she sips a bottle of beer tentatively while adjusting oxygen tubes in her nose.

Kate's eyes brighten when she notices Hannah in the crowd. "Hannah!" Kate waves her over and gives her a hug. The smiling Kate talks slowly and unnecessarily loudly. "I didn't think you were coming tonight. Where's your—"

Hannah shakes her head and cuts off Kate mid-sentence. "I need to find Jack," she says at a volume that's barely heard above the party din. "Uncle Sam needs him."

"What's that?" Kate puts up a hand to one ear, an oversized diamond ring catching the light. She turns to the woman in the gold dress beside her. "Ariel, this is Jack's partner's niece, Hannah. You met her uncle, Sam, at your baby shower."

Ariel smiles. "Ah, yes." She reaches out a hand to Hannah. "Your uncle came to visit me just today."

Hannah looks at Ariel's French manicured hand and shakes it quickly. She turns back to Kate. Hannah touches her fingertips to her throat to get a better feel for the volume and yells. "Where is Jack? Sam needs him. Emergency."

At the word "emergency" the old lady in the wheelchair looks up at Hannah.

The band's spiky-haired guitar player takes the stage and grabs the microphone. "Check, check, one-two." The sound of his voice is amplified and joined by a few tuning strokes on the electric guitar.

"Jack's at the bar getting drinks." Kate has to yell to be heard but remembers too late Hannah is only reading lips. Kate points to one of the cocktail bars erected near the sitting area of the atrium, along the wide front windows that face the city streets. The long, temporary tables are swamped with patrons waving drink tickets at the bartenders, who hustle to serve wine, beer, and one-mixer cocktails to the demanding crowd.

"Is everything okay?" Ariel asks Kate.

Kate shrugs. "Not sure." Kate taps Hannah on the shoulder and turns her back around. "Is Sam okay? Can I help?"

"He was arrested," Hannah says. Simultaneously she signs, "In jail," but Kate doesn't follow. Hannah tries again. "Sam needs to warn Jack about someone named Paulo."

Ariel's eyes dart from the stage to Hannah. "Did you say Paulo?"

Hannah nods and heads toward the bar.

Ariel pulls out her phone and dials. She scans the crowded room for ushers wearing the maroon Raptor Institute shirts as Paulo's voicemail greeting plays.

"Everything okay?" Kate shouts over the din to Ariel.

Ariel shakes her head. "I don't know. Paulo was supposed to be here by now, but I don't see him." Ariel ends the call.

Outside in the car, Sara chews on her lip and reloads the email app on her smart phone. She flips through Sam's briefcase and pulls out what she's looking for—fire department employment records.

The detective seemed skeptical about her abilities when he'd called. She'd prefer to be in her office at the university where she had proper lighting and scanning equipment. In order to provide an accurate assessment, she really needed the physical letter—it was much more informative than a photo, since pen pressure and other factors were critical to an accurate identification.

Sara hadn't met any of the people involved in Sam's research, but she'd heard about Conrad, Paulo, and Ariel many times as Sam had shown her his files—always ending in a frustrated rant with nothing but dead ends to show for his efforts. She wasn't sure what Sam had found out today about Paulo or how it may be related to his apparent suicide, but if Sam needed her help now, she'd do her best.

Finally, a message from the police department pops up on her phone. Sara opens the email attachment—a scanned PDF of Paulo's scribbled suicide note. It's small on the phone screen, but she uses her thumb and forefinger to zoom in. She reads it carefully, line by line.

Sara flicks her gaze back and forth between the tiny phone screen and a job application on the passenger seat. The fire department paperwork has several samples of Paulo's writing throughout. She carefully compares the documents from Sam's files with the suicide note.

I don't regret making the terrorists pay.

She notes the long crosses of the *t*'s and checks them against Paulo's employment application. She compares the spacing of the words and slant of the letters.

She sighs and looks through the car window at the stream of patrons entering the atrium, now slowing as the event is fully underway. Sara pulls off her glasses, confused. It's not a match.

60

Hannah approaches the crowded bar, searching for any sign of Jack's ruddy face, brown hair, or big belly. No dice. She catches Travis's eye near the restroom area. He signs that he's going to check out the bird hospital and storeroom area in the back and walks down the dimly lit hallway. She beckons him to join her near the bar, but he can't see clearly through the crowd and continues on his way toward the back hallway.

Hannah turns back toward the crowd. Her eyes land on a laughing set of blue eyes she recognizes. It's Jack.

⚭

In the car, Sara rolls her neck from shoulder to shoulder and thinks. Her eyes land on an array of files and papers from Sam's briefcase strewn across the front seat. Newspaper articles, insurance policy paperwork, and fire department forms clutter the surface.

She readies her cell to call the detective with her analysis on the note but stops short as her eyes land on a second file folder buried under the pile. She flips it open. Inside, she finds a copy of a handwritten affidavit regarding the first arson incident—the Ahzartec explosion that had killed Alex. Sara recalls Sam pouring over the reports from everyone on the scene after his sister's death, including all the first responders. She pulls the paper from the stack and scans the signature. She closely inspects the loopy letter *C* in the name. She holds the signature up to the suicide note on her phone screen. The *C* in *Consuela* is a perfect match.

"Oh, shit," she whispers.

Sara freezes, imagining the truth—Conrad Bane Jr., in heavy black boots, stands outside the Ahzartec building and presses a button on a cell phone. The building explodes. Conrad walks away unseen from the smoking rubble of Senator Bergen's office as sirens approach. In the hotel stairwell, Conrad bars the door to the sixth-floor exit. Conrad scribbles a fake suicide note. The note is false, but the sentiments are real. Conrad's father was a beloved man—whose life was cut short by his duty to a city under attack—and whose memory was mocked by politicians, lawyers, and businesses who spat in the face of all he stood for.

"Hannah!" Sara opens the car door, panicked. She runs inside, dialing the contact number she has saved for Detective Kelly. She leaves a message as a group of high-heeled young women exit the coatroom at the same time Sara enters through the heavy, rotating door.

The pack of women smash into Sara, knocking the phone from her hand. It skitters toward an open section of rotating door, and is carried outside by another party coming in. Sara starts towards the door but lets it go as a rush of patrons— laughing—gets stuck in the cubicle.

"Shit," she mutters but continues into the atrium. She'll grab it once she gets Hannah safely out of the building and away from any possible danger. Conrad may be somewhere inside, the "old friends" attending the party with Jack and Kate, according to Hannah.

Sara rushes into the atrium and scans the crowd. Hannah is looking for Jack. If Hannah mentions Paulo in front of Conrad, and Conrad had something to do with Paulo's death, then Hannah could be in grave danger. Sara pushes into the crowd and looks frantically for Hannah's spiky silver and purple hair. *Where is she?*

The eighties cover band strikes its first chord, and the entire crowd pushes toward the stage as the sound of new-wave electronica fills the atrium with ear-piercing keyboard and guitar riffs.

"Hannah!" Sara calls in futility—both because the band's music crescendos into a deafening roar and because Hannah cannot hear her screams.

Sara scans the crowd and sees Kate frantically waving her over. Sara pushes her way through dancing patrons over to Kate. "Hannah?" Sara pants.

Kate points toward the bar area. Although she speaks loudly, Sara can barely hear over the roar of the electric guitar. "She's looking for Jack. She said Sam needs him urgently."

Sara nods in agreement. "Kate, I'll explain later, but please be careful tonight. I know Conrad Bane is your friend, but there's information that I just found out and—"

Before Sara can finish her sentence, Kate cuts her off and gestures to Ariel, who stands next to her. Mrs. Bane glares up at Sara from her wheelchair and breathes loudly through the oxygen tubes in her nose.

Kate shouts. "This is Ariel Bane. She's married to Conrad." Kate looks pointedly at Sara to allow this to sink in. "As you know, Jack and Connie go way back. Very old friends."

Sara looks at Ariel and Candy, who both glare at her in confusion. Sara is not sure whether they heard what she said. Her heart skips a beat, and she wonders where Conrad is at this moment, but she doesn't ask.

Ariel holds her stomach with one hand and wipes beads of sweat from her brow. "Paulo, my cousin, he's supposed to be here. Jack and Sam were trying to talk to him earlier today. Do you know why?"

Sara has the urge to explain what's happened to Paulo, but she hesitates. Clearly, the news of Paulo's death has not yet reached the family.

"Sara, Ariel is very worried about her cousin, Paulo," Kate says. "She's starting to panic. He was supposed to work here tonight."

"My husband is also not here. Connie told me to come on ahead with Candy," Ariel says. "That he needed to work late at the station." Her brow is furrowed in what is now grave concern for both men. "Candy and I came ahead. I thought I would see them both here." She flips over the bejeweled case of her iPhone. "It's very late now. I am worried and neither of them answers. I am not to feel . . . feeling dizzy . . ." Ariel's cell phone drops from her hand onto the floor, and she doubles over in pain.

Mrs. Bane cringes at a loud guitar riff and plugs her ears. Ignoring her daughter-in-law's distress, she rolls the wheels of her chair away from the stage and toward the back of the large room, near the wall separating the bird hospital from the atrium.

Kate rushes to catch Ariel. "Ariel? Are you okay?" She turns to Sara. "Help me."

Sara steps forward and helps to steady a wobbly Ariel. She and Kate move the moaning woman away from the stage to a bench near Mrs. Bane, who is trying to turn herself away from the wall she now faces in the chair.

"There," Kate shouts over the music as they sit Ariel on a bench. She points to Hannah's purple-tinted hair just visible near the bar. "Hannah's over there."

Ariel leans against the wall, panting. Her eyes are filled with tears. "What's happened to Paulo?" Ariel holds her stomach and cringes in pain.

"Kate, you should get her outside. I think Ariel and the baby may be in distress." Sara starts toward the bar. "I need to get Hannah, but you should get her to the hospital."

"Wait, I need Connie. W-w-where is he?" Ariel stammers.

Kate nods and helps Ariel to her feet. "We'll find him. Let's get a breath of fresh air." Ariel and Kate head for the front entrance.

As Sara heads toward the bar area, Candy Bane grabs her arm. Candy's sharp fingernails cut into Sara's skin. Sara jerks her arm away. "What the hell?"

Candy croaks, "Why were you warning Jack's wife about my Connie? What do you know about my son?"

"Nothing," Sara says. She bolts toward the bar.

Candy Bane watches Sara disappear into the sea of tall bar tables and party guests.

As Hannah pushes her way toward the bar, she waves a hand to catch Jack's attention. She generates a guttural wail in her throat, frustrated, as Jack laughs at something the bartender says. He's oblivious to her. Hannah's phone vibrates in her pocket. She pulls it out and reads a text from Travis.

Locked out. Come open the security door and let me back in. Past bird hospital, through storeroom, on the right.

With a last look at Jack, now chatting up the bartender, Hannah heads toward the restrooms and down the hallway. At that moment, Sara sees Hannah and calls out over the crowd. Again, she realizes too late that Hannah cannot hear her. She reaches into the empty pocket of her jeans for her cell phone. "Shit," Sara says, recalling its whereabouts on the sidewalk somewhere outside. She follows Hannah down the hallway.

62

Jimmy jogs up to the holding cell. "We heard from Sara." Detective Kelly joins them and taps the voicemail entry on his phone.

"The note is a fake," Sara's voice is breathless. "Paulo's letter is *not* in his handwriting. It's a match to Conrad Bane Jr. . . . I matched it to his handwritten affidavit. Sam had his office send over copies of all police and firefighter files when he was investigating Ahzartec. . . . Oh my God—what if he's here? Hannah is in there trying to find Jack—call you back."

The line goes dead.

Sam's face is instantly white. "What's . . . where are they? Where is Hannah? Is she okay?"

"Sam, we're going to search now," Detective Kelly says. "We *will* find them. Jimmy, put out an APB on Conrad Bane Jr."

Jimmy nods and heads for a brunette officer sitting at a nearby desk. She takes down the details of the request.

Sam clasps the bars and yells, "Let me out, please, Detective!"

"When your lawyer gets here, Sam. Our hands are tied, but we're going to your house first. We'll call back in as soon as we find them." Detective Kelly waves for Jimmy.

"But Sara said they were going in somewhere to find Jack. Did you reach him?" Sam says in a high voice, pinched with tension.

"No answer on Jack's or Sara's cell phones," Jimmy says, approaching Detective Kelly.

"My cell!" Sam says instantly. "Hannah shares her location with me."

Detective Kelly nods at Jimmy, who returns a few minutes later with Sam's phone. Sam boots it up, enters the passcode, and selects the location sharing app. He jiggles a knee in anticipation as the little dot on the map blinks. Its location is on the cross streets where Sam is standing. At the police station.

"This is *my* phone," Sam grunts. "Where's hers? It shows we're sharing locations but it's not showing me where her phone is." Sam curses in frustration. He checks the connectivity bars on his phone; they're down to one.

"Sometimes those location sharing apps time out. Happens to me all the time," Jimmy says. "Plus, the service inside this building is nearly nonexistent. We tried to text her with an emergency message, but no reply."

"Can't you just track her phone . . . or Jack's . . . or Sara's? GPS or something?" Sam asks.

Jimmy smiles woefully. "We can get historical data with no warrant, but nothing real-time without a judge's order."

"We need to go, Sam." Detective Kelly holds out a hand. Sam reluctantly pushes his cell phone back through the bars. Detective Kelly returns the device to Officer Brewer and follows Jimmy down the hallway and out of sight.

Sam kicks the cell door in frustration. The bars rattle like a death knell.

63

Hannah passes the darkened bird hospital as she makes her way toward the storeroom to let Travis back inside. The hospital is empty, and only the dim green light of computer screen savers illuminates the abandoned bird cages and medical equipment. Hannah smiles. The injured birds must have been relocated to the Raptor Institute's alternate hospital facility north of the city.

She enters the storeroom. It's dimly lit with most of the light coming from the bright-red exit sign above the heavy security door and a dim overhead fixture that's missing a bulb. She passes a wall of cleaning supplies, paper products, and bird feed. On the back wall to the right of the heavy metal security door, she reads a sign.

Opening door will sound alarm.

She hesitates for a moment. Certainly, the security system has been disabled for the party. She shoves the push bar of the door open with a hip and braces for blinking lights or the appearance of an alarm, but nothing happens.

Across the alleyway, Travis sits on a low wall near a large garbage bin. She waves at him, but his head remains bowed. His fingers flick across the screen of his phone, playing a game.

She steps out into the night air and waves with one hand while holding the locking security door open with the other. She pulls out her phone, ready to text him to get his attention. Before she can finish, everything goes black.

64

Ted, Adelaar's in-house council and Sam's personal lawyer, approaches Sam's cell in a college basketball jersey. He's winded. "Sam! I'm so sorry. I was at the game. I'm trying to find a judge that will release you tonight."

Sam slumps onto a metal bench against the cell wall.

The brunette officer sitting across from the holding cell approaches Sam and Ted. "Mr. Abernethy, your house checked out okay—nothing was amiss, but your niece and Miss Parker were not there."

Sam sighs heavily.

Ted turns to the officer and holds out a hand. "Thanks, Officer . . ."

"Brewer."

Ted nods. "Officer Brewer, thanks for keeping us posted. We appreciate it very much."

"You've got to find them!" Sam calls to Officer Brewer as she returns to her desk. "Tell Jimmy and Detective Kelly that I don't know what Conrad is capable of or if he even knows Sara discovered his handwriting on the note . . . but if he is behind these arson attacks . . . if he's the one who killed Alex . . . " Sam bites his lip and pleads with the officer. "Please, Officer Brewer, please tell Jimmy to make sure my girls are safe. I can't lose anyone else."

"I'll tell them, sir." Officer Brewer nods reassuringly.

Ted removes a ball cap and scratches thin gray hair. "I've called in a favor. Hold tight, Sam. We're going to get you out of here."

"Ted, can I borrow your phone?" Sam reaches through the bars.

Ted shrugs quizzically and hands it over.

೧೦

Sam looks up as someone approaches his cell.

Dr. Indy Patel skates in wearing a large backpack. He rolls to a stop in front of Sam's cell and pushes a button on the side of each sneaker to retract the wheels.

"Did you have trouble getting in?" Sam asks through the bars.

Indy pops his gum and shakes his head. "No. It's usually the getting out of this place that's a problem. Not the getting in." He grins widely and unzips his pack. After pulling up a desk chair from a nearby workstation, he starts to work.

In a few minutes, Sam is hooked up to Indy's neurotheology helmet through the cell bars. Wires connect it to a laptop computer.

"I didn't think you were a fan of my methods," Indy says, entering a password at the laptop's log-in screen.

Sam paces, adjusting the bulky helmet around his ears. Officer Brewer, against her better judgment, had opened the cell to allow Sam to access the device.

"The letters, the connection you talked about. I need to talk to Alex," Sam says.

Indy looks at Sam skeptically but says nothing. He hits the enter key, and the magnets connected to the laptop spin to life.

Sam fidgets. He scans the walls expectantly. Indy scans the laptop monitor.

Sam sits on the metal bench in his cell and closes his eyes. A little girl's laughter rings through his ears. His own voice calls out, "Alex . . ." The memories fade into echo.

Outside the cell, Indy checks his watch. "Now, we wait." He stretches out his legs and crosses them.

Sam searches his mind for Alex. He thinks about her as hard as he can, but nothing happens. He feels no connection and sees no images. He hears the magnets whirring in the helmet, but this time it's just noise.

Moments later, the computer program ends. The magnets spin down. Sam wearily removes the helmet from his head and detaches the electrodes stuck to his temples. "I don't understand. Nothing happened," he says.

Officer Brewer opens the cell door, retrieves the helmet, and hands it back to Indy.

"Thanks." Indy deposits the equipment into the backpack.

"Well?" Sam blurts. "What gives? Why didn't it work this time?"

"I'm sorry, Sam. But this isn't a key to unlock every door, man. It's a gift. And one that I have yet to truly understand."

Sam kicks the metal bench in his cell, causing a loud clatter. Officer Brewer turns to address it, but Indy holds up a hand, and she nods, standing down.

"A gift?" Sam snorts. "What good is this shit if it doesn't work when I need it to? Hannah is out there. And Sara . . . They could be in trouble, and I'm stuck in here, totally useless!"

Indy says, "Sam, it's okay. It's gonna—"

Sam yells at the top of his voice, almost growling. "Goddamn it, Alex, you talk to me, you hear me?! You talk to me!"

Sam breaks down, head in hands. His eyes flood with unshed tears.

Ted rushes in from the hallway, breathless. "You made bail, Sam." Ted waves over Officer Brewer. "Can you help?" He hands her the paperwork.

Sam wastes no time. He wipes his eyes and hangs on the cell door. "Get me outta here."

65

Alex

I have been really distracted lately. I have let Sam down. I haven't been able to get to the construction zone for a while.

Guess who visited me? That's right—Mom and Dad. They were together, and they were young. Like how I remember them from before the accident. Dad went on and on about the dangers of the construction zone. He thinks it's bad for me to be there. Mom thinks if I can help Sam and Hannah, I should do it. They both told me I don't have very long. They said that my time here will soon end, one way or the other. They said they'd be waiting for me, and I should get things wrapped up. I am not sure what to do. I feel a strong pull to join my parents, but my heart is with Sam and Hannah still.

When I approach the construction zone to consider everything, I know immediately something is very wrong. My insides churn like a washing machine, and I feel instantly sick. I can't see clearly, but I know without a doubt my daughter is in trouble. And Sam is lost in the dark.

I think about the eagles I sent Hannah.

Sam runs out of the police station as Ted jogs behind him. "Wait up, Sam!" Ted calls. "I'll drive you home."

Sam surveys Center City and pants, hands on his knees. All is dark and silent. A few passersby scurry away from him.

Ted catches up, breathing hard. "Sam, Officer Brewer stopped me on the way out. They didn't find Hannah at her school. They haven't located Bane yet either. They urged me to take you home in case Hannah and Sara show up there."

Sam shakes his head. "I can't sit and do nothing. Can you give me a ride?"

Ted nods and unlocks his sleek car with a beep.

⍧

Sam hops out of the car in front of the darkened university building. Ted checks his watch.

"Sam, I'm sorry. I can't wait."

"It's okay, Ted." Sam walks toward Sara's building.

"But what if they're not here?" Ted yells after him.

Sam puts up a hand in goodbye. "I've got to try something." He runs.

At the dimly lit criminology building, Sam jiggles the glass doors, but they are locked. He bangs on them, gritting his teeth. "Sara! Hannah! Are you in there?"

Sam calls Sara for the fifth time. It rings into Sara's voicemail. "Hello, you've reached the phone of Doctor Sara Parker. Please leave a message—"

Sam hangs up and dials Jack. As it has been doing all night, the call goes instantly to voicemail. Jack's voicemail greeting plays. "You've reached Jack. If you're a hot babe, leave a message. If not, who needs ya?"

Jack's phone is clearly turned off. Sam calls Hannah's phone again, but there's no answer. Sam knows if Hannah were available, his call would appear to her as captions on her phone screen and she would type a response to him—they use the phone captioning app all the time. He hangs up and jams the phone back in his pocket.

"Shit," Sam mutters. He wanders aimlessly around the campus, his heart thumping so loudly he is sure other people can hear it. He knows this effort is futile; he knows Detective Kelly and Jimmy are searching for Sara and Hannah, and that the smart play would be to head home and wait.

He racks his brain. Sam knows Sara retrieved Hannah from school because he saw a text confirming so. Next thing he heard was Sara's frantic voicemail warning about Conrad and his handwriting being a match to Paulo's supposed suicide note. Where was Sara calling from? Where on earth would she be concerned that Hannah would somehow run into Conrad?

Sam's panic escalates irrationally. He runs up to the closest building, a student dormitory, and bangs on its locked doors. He yells and peeks through dark windows. He stops a student in a beanie cap. "Do you know Dr. Sara Parker? Have you seen her? She's a criminology professor?"

"No," the student says. The young man steps backward as he notices Sam's darkened eyes, sweaty skin, and wilted clothing.

Sam yells into the darkness. "For God's sake, Alex. HELP ME!"

The beanie-capped student jogs away immediately.

Sam begins to run through the wooded campus, yelling "Sara" and "Hannah" into the darkness. Before he reaches the next dorm building, he trips over a gray lump on the sidewalk and stumbles to the ground. His chin bursts open on the concrete, splattering blood. A woman shrieks behind him. As Sam turns to look, the gray lump rises from the sidewalk and unfolds as a fur-clad homeless woman.

She beats on Sam's back with her tattered purse. "Watch where you're going, you psycho!"

Sam sighs heavily and wipes blood from his chin. He rolls into a sitting position on the sidewalk, defeated and exhausted. "I'm sorry."

The homeless woman, shocked at the direct attention, squeals and scurries away from him. She mumbles, "Watch where you're going!"

Sam yells back, "I wish I knew where I was going! I am completely lost."

The homeless woman yells back from the darkness, her voice moving farther away each second like a train horn receding down the track. "There are signs all around you. Signs all around you!" And then she's gone.

For a split second, Sam's déjà vu is overwhelming. He's back in Madame Amanda's strange reading room with the wooden mask, its white eyes staring down at him. Madame Amanda pops her gum loudly and says in her sweet Southern drawl, "Just take a look around, sweetie. There are signs all around you."

Sam is suddenly wide awake. He looks up to see a nearby lamppost covered with flyers directly in front of him. A neon-pink poster catches his eye. He stares at it. Suddenly, everywhere he looks, the same sign appears, stapled on lampposts, taped on newspaper stands, hung in windows.

In blue, purple, green, pink, and yellow, posters of bald eagles are pinned all over campus. How did he not see this before?

Hannah's paintings of multicolored bald eagles flash before Sam's eyes. The eagles are a perfect match. Sam rushes to the poster on the lamppost.

NORTH CAROLINA RAPTOR INSTITUTE BIRDS
OF PREY FUNDRAISER TONIGHT FEATURING
AWESOME 80S COVER BAND—SAVED BY THE YELL
DON'T MISS IT! IT'S JUST WHAT
YOU'RE LOOKING FOR!

Sam runs.

67

Sara enters the storeroom. She scans the shadowy corners. Her eyes take a moment to adjust to the dim lighting. She starts to call out, "Hannah?" but catches herself.

A slightly muffled bass rhythm vibrates the walls as Sara scans shelving loaded with large bags of feed, spray bottles of yellow cleaning solution, and cardboard boxes stacked six feet high marked with graphics of paper towels and toilet rolls.

Sara halts upon hearing a sound. "Hello?" She takes a tentative step farther into the room and hears the sound again. It's a low moan. Suddenly, the top two cardboard boxes, full of paper towels, tip from the top of the stack and bounce on the floor. Sara jumps back, startled.

Now visible in the corner, Hannah sits on the floor, hands and feet zip-tied together. A small trickle of blood runs down her forehead. She is awake but gagged with a black plastic trash bag. Her eyes are wide. She nods at something in the corner of the room and moans again.

Sara rushes toward her, alarmed. As she bends down to help, the unmistakable click of a gun being cocked emanates from somewhere behind her. Sara freezes.

68

Sam approaches a bright-pink copy of the eagle promo poster, which is pinned to a utility pole on the cross streets of the Raptor Institute's downtown atrium location. Streetlights buzz overhead as he peers through the same large picture window he had seen the previous week during his visit with Paulo.

Inside the multistory atrium, now aglow with myriad colored lights, partygoers crowd near a stage where a group of musicians in spiky wigs and tight jeans jump and play a headbanging classic. He looks for Hannah and Sara, but patrons exiting the event—many of them clearly tipsy—make it impossible to identify them from outside.

Sam heads toward the entrance of the atrium and breathes a sigh of relief as a valet parking attendant hands Kate a set of keys.

"Kate!" Sam yells. He kicks himself inwardly. He should have recalled that Jack and Kate were heading to the Raptor Institute's fundraising event tonight. They had begged him and Hannah to join them, but Sam had declined. He should have realized that Sara may have come here searching for Jack.

Because *he* had asked her to find him. Hannah would have known where they were. Sam should have remembered that and not wasted so much time. *Shit.*

Sam jogs toward Kate, who navigates a crowd of exiting partygoers and helps Ariel into her SUV. Kate is having a hard time fitting Ariel's puffy gold dress into the car. Sam pants. "Hannah—is she here?"

Kate nods back toward the atrium. Sam sighs heavily. *Thank God.*

Ariel recognizes Sam and rolls down the back window. "Sam! Where's Connie? I'm having the baby."

Shocked, Sam doesn't know what to say. "Kate, Ariel . . . you should go to the hospital now."

Ariel holds her big stomach and grimaces in pain.

"Breathe," Kate says, rounding the car. "I'm coming."

"Wait!" Ariel searches Sam's face. "Sam, what's happened to Paulo? What do you know?"

Sam hesitates but says nothing. He knows now is not the time to explain.

"Why were you coming to talk to him today?" Ariel's brown eyes are desperate. "Paulo never showed up here. Something is wrong."

"I'm sorry, Ariel. You need to get to the hospital now. I'll have the police call you there."

"Police?" Ariel's face blanches. "What? Why?"

Sam calls to Kate, now in the driver's seat. "Kate, you need to go *now.*"

Kate nods and speeds off into the night.

As Sam rushes toward the atrium's entrance, he sees Sara's silver sedan parked in a small area behind the valet stand.

☙

As he enters the atrium, Sam passes the darkened Raptor Institute gift shop near the front entrance and spots Jack some distance away, near the bar. A shaft of moonlight from the glass atrium ceiling illuminates a thinning crowd of patrons as the night winds down.

A perched hawk screeches shrilly high above Sam's head as the pierced lead singer of the band says, "And that's our set, folks. Follow us online at dub-dub-dub-saved-by-yell-dot-com." The guitar player throws in one last shrill whine of the strings, and the band closes out with a loud pound of the drums.

Sam moves quickly through a gaggle of cheering patrons and staff members tumbling empty plastic drinkware and cocktail napkins into trash bags.

Sam reaches Jack as the bartender calls out, "Last call, folks. You don't have to go home, but . . . you know the rest."

A few moans of disappointment come from the die-hard drinking crowd as Jack sees Sam. "Sam, you made it!" He raises a hand toward the bartender. "What'll you have? It's last call."

Sam shakes his head violently. "Have you seen Hannah and Sara?"

"What?" Jack doesn't compute. "I didn't think you guys were coming. I've been waiting to meet up with Connie, but he never showed up."

"Paulo's dead, Jack. I've been calling you all night. Conrad may be part of all this."

Jack's face, ruddy from drinking, is instantly drained of color. He sets his highball down on the bar. "Part of what?"

"Sara? Hannah?" Sam repeats.

Jack shakes his head, dazedly. "No, I haven't seen them." He looks across the expansive room toward the band, now breaking down all their equipment. "Kate may have. She's over there somewhere."

Sam spins around the room, checking the crowd. He sees a tall, spectacled man in a tuxedo step out of the bathrooms. He recalls the tour Paulo had given him and Jack just a week ago. "I'm going to check the back by the bird hospital. I'll explain later. Be careful." Sam moves quickly but calls over his shoulder. "Call Kate—she had to take Ariel to the emergency room."

"Be careful of what? My phone's in the car," Jack shouts.

Sam waves him off and bolts toward the hallway near the restrooms. Jack downs the last of his whiskey in one gulp.

69

Sam yells into the ladies' room. "Sara! Are you in there?"

A little girl in a black velvet dress squeals in fright as Sam's head pokes through the swinging door.

"Sorry," he says.

He passes the darkened bird hospital and sees through the picture windows that there's no human or fowl inside. He approaches the storeroom—which he knows leads to the back door.

He hears voices and calls out, "Sara?"

"Sam!" Sara bellows from inside. "Help!"

Sam opens the door and is immediately struck on the head by something heavy. He tumbles to the floor. The back of his head throbs, and his vision tunnels to black for a second. The gray concrete floor sways like a lava lamp as he tries to steady himself.

He looks up to see a blurry figure coming in and out of focus—a silver mane atop a weathered face. Candy Bane sits in her wheelchair, wheezing loudly through oxygen tubes in her nose.

Sam tries to right himself, but he is dizzy. "What the—"

Hannah moans from the corner. She sits back-to-back with Sara on the floor. Both have their hands and feet bound with zip ties.

"Hannah!" Sam lurches toward his niece, but Candy raises the pistol. Sam freezes, confused.

"The girl is fine," Candy wheezes with a nod toward Hannah. "She came tearing into the party warning us about Paulo. And this one"—she nods at Sara—"came in raving nonsense about my Connie. When I followed the girl back here and asked her what she knew, she wouldn't answer me. But, luckily, your girlfriend here showed up"—Candy gestures at Sara with the slim, black pistol—"and let me know about the lies. The lies she told the police about my Connie."

"She's crazy, Sam." Sara stammers. "When I matched the handwriting on Paulo's suicide note to Conrad, I came inside looking for Hannah—it's my fault, I sent her in here to get Jack—I'm so sorry." Sara's pupils are dilated in the dim light, giving her the appearance of a stunned cat. She turns wildly to Candy and yells, "I told you Hannah is deaf! She couldn't hear you to answer your questions, you crazy—"

Candy shoots. The bullet whizzes over Sara's head—very close—and into the drywall behind her. "I told you to *shut up*, or I'll gag you too."

Hannah's eyes are wide with shock. Sara's eyes are saucers. Sam wonders if anyone in the atrium heard the shot.

Candy reaches into a saddlebag on the side of her wheelchair and pulls out a double-looped plastic zip tie and tosses it to Sam. "Put this on. And don't be cute."

Sam locks eyes with Hannah. *I'll get you out of here.* He tries to convey the message the best he can with a look as he slips his hands into the plastic cuffs and pulls the leads. For a split second, he wonders why an old woman would have zip ties in her bag.

"Tighter, please," Candy wheezes. She smiles, pleased. "Connie has lots of friends in the police department. Yeah, they love him there. They know he comes from a long line of heroes, he does."

Sam shifts to his knees and turns toward Candy, palms up. "Mrs. Bane, I am sorry that Conrad got you involved with this, but you've got to get your son some help." He nods to Hannah and Sara. "Let them go. No one else needs to get hurt. The police are looking for Conrad now. This will be over soon."

"Yes. It will," Candy hisses. "Fires start all the time due to incompetence. Cleaning solution, old batteries, the dropped cigarette. Usually, it's the staff in a place like this. Sneaking a drink or a smoke around all this flammable liquid. Idiots, really."

With her free hand, Candy flips open the silver top of a butane lighter. It illuminates the storeroom in wild, uneven light. Candy holds the lighter in one hand, and the gun in the other.

Sam notices a stream of sparkling liquid on the floor beneath Candy's wheelchair. It is only now that Sam notices the empty bottle of ammonia cleaning solution tossed aside on the floor.

"What are you doing?!" he screams.

"Twenty-seven years as the wife of a firefighter, you learn a couple things," Candy says, admiring the flaming lighter in her hand.

"What the hell? Candy! Put that out! You'll burn us all!" Sam yells.

Candy points to the sprinklers. "Like how arsonists tamper with the sprinkler systems"—she wheezes and points to the open hallway door—"or how an open door accelerates a soaked subfloor with the tiniest of sparks."

She smiles at the flame and drops it.

70

Jack makes his way to a bench near the entrance of the atrium. He's one of a few patrons left. The staff members finish cleaning and haul the last bags of trash outside through a side entrance. Jack reaches into his pocket to call Kate but realizes his phone is in the glove box of their SUV. His mind is fuzzy with bourbon. He didn't sleep very well last night—the damn next-door neighbors were blasting tunes until at least two o'clock in the morning. He tries to focus. He thinks Sam said Kate was taking Ariel to have the baby. He thinks about how he'll get to the hospital without a phone. Do cabs still troll Uptown picking up bar-hoppers? He hopes so but isn't sure in the age of ride-sharing apps.

Jack takes a deep breath and enjoys the emptiness of the huge atrium. He wonders how long it will take for building security guards to kick him out. Maybe he'll just rest a minute until he can figure out how to get home. He wonders where Sam went. He recalls he went toward the restrooms. Maybe he should find him? Sam seemed a little distracted. He'll find him. In a minute.

Jack lies down on the bench and closes his eyes.

71

In the storeroom, Candy drops the lighter to the floor.

"No!" Sam wails.

Within seconds, the line of cleaning fluid ignites, becoming a ring of fire that snakes through the storeroom and surrounds them.

Sam is bewildered. Panic and fear rise in his throat. His lips tighten in fury, and he launches himself from his knees toward the old woman in the chair.

Candy buckles as Sam's head slams into her face. She spits out an angry yell as her false teeth rattle and pop out of her mouth and land on the floor. Sam shudders at the sight.

Breathless and toothless, Candy wheezes under Sam's weight but maneuvers her right arm out from under him. She sticks the pistol in his belly. He freezes and rolls off her, hitting the floor hard.

Candy cackles and admires the gun. "They said this wasn't an appropriate gift for my grandson. Maybe they were right."

Sara screams as flames lick the toes of her shoes. She and Hannah shift and scoot away from the fire into the back corner inch by inch. It's all they can manage with their limited range of motion.

Smoke rises from the burning boxes of paper products and bags of feed that surround them. Above their heads, sprinklers click on and life-saving droplets begin to fall upon their heads. The fire alarm blares.

Candy takes aim—she shoots the room's sprinkler clean off the pipe. Somehow, the fitting remains intact and stems the flow of water from the pipes, but no more water falls onto the growing fire.

The flames rage within seconds, feeding on the ammonia and alcohol in the cleaning solution and consuming paper products in seconds. Sam and Sara choke on thick smoke. Hannah's face is ashen. She can barely breathe and chokes on her plastic gag.

Sam awkwardly rises again and takes two wide steps toward the old woman. Unexpectedly, Candy stands and shoots, sending a bullet whizzing just over Sam's head. He drops back down to the floor and rolls onto his side awkwardly.

"You can walk?" he says, dazed.

Candy wheezes from the effort and falls back into her wheelchair. "When it's warranted. For a few minutes. Those goddamn hotel stairs nearly killed me, though."

Scenes flash through Sam's mind. Candy sits in her wheel-chair, in heavy black boots, outside the Ahzartec building and presses a button on a cell phone. The building explodes. Candy, walking unsteadily, places a silver eagle charm next to the entrance, falls back into a wheelchair, and rolls away. Later, at Senator Bergen's office, the old woman's gloved hand gently places the owl charm near the door in the smoking rubble of the office. At the hotel, Candy, in a firefighter mask, drops a silver falcon outside the lobby of the hotel as flames erupt behind her.

Sam's eyes water with rage. He shouts, "You killed Alex! You hurt those kids!"

Candy yells, "No! The hotel was an accident. The lawyers were supposed to be there." The old woman rolls herself past Sam toward the open door to the hallway. The fire alarm is in full effect now. Emergency lights blink all the way up the corridor.

Sam struggles against his plastic zip ties, but his hands are not budging. He looks up at Candy from the floor. "You need help, Candy. I can help you. We have resources. Just let my family go. They're innocent."

Candy scoffs loudly, "Ha!" This act causes her weak lungs to react, and she spasms in a coughing fit. Somewhere outside, Sam hears the distant wailing of a siren.

Before Sam can launch at her again, Candy tightens her grip on the gun and spins her wheelchair around. She breathes openmouthed, her bare gums like a teething baby. Finally, she replies, "Innocent? Who is innocent? The terrorists who killed my husband? The bastard lawyers who stole my settlement money and screwed the survivors? The senator who approved the sale of Ahzartec to a Saudi billionaire who they've proven has laundered money for al-Qaeda? No one is innocent."

"Conrad Jr. will take the fall for this—you know that, don't you? If you let us go now, I'll get you and Conrad the help you need. I'll explain to the police that you helped us, that you saved us, Candy."

Candy stops in her tracks. Framing the tiny, white-haired old woman in her wheelchair, flames scurry up the doorjamb.

Behind her, in the hallway, white-hot flames begin to eat through a wooden bench near the entrance to the bird hospital.

She addresses Sam. "You are stupid, aren't you? Just as stupid as Paulo. I told Connie not to get involved with those people. The Colombians are just as bad as the terrorists." She points the gun at Sam. "Paulo was itching to leave this world anyway—what with his fiancée killed as she was. He told me so once."

Candy smiles and cranks up the oxygen on her tank. "He thought I liked him, for heaven's sake." She breathes in a long breath of clean oxygen. "It didn't take more than a peace offering of his favorite brand of tequila, infused with a bottle of my pills, of course, to do the job he didn't have the balls to do: to leave the pain of this world behind."

Candy nods at nothing in particular. "The bird charms should have been enough. But the cops were too stupid to put it together." She eyes Sam critically. "I had to help them along. The police are discovering all the evidence they need at Paulo's house, probably right now. Plans for the Queen City Hotel building, replicas of the ignition device used in Senator Bergen's office. Regardless of what that bitch thinks she knows about a scribbled note written by a mental case"—Candy whips the gun toward Sara—"the police will realize that it all adds up and points to Paulo." Candy sweeps the burning room with a last look. "And whatever else you may be inclined to share about our little meeting here tonight . . . well, that will go up in smoke in a few minutes, won't it?"

Candy begins to roll down the smoke-filled hallway and yells back to Sam, "Your sister was an unfortunate casualty. Just like my husband. You and I are both the losers here, Sam."

72

In the atrium, Jack stirs as the fire alarm blares. He looks around. Everyone else has left the building. He hears fire sirens approaching but sees nothing ablaze. Then he smells it. Smoke floats down the hallway near the restrooms and spreads into the atrium like a menacing fog. He looks up to see a creeper of an orange flame in the corner of the wall that separates the atrium from the bird hospital and storeroom.

"Shit," Jack says, now wide awake.

Candy Bane rolls into the atrium. For a moment, Jack is disoriented. Where did she come from? He had seen her earlier in the night but had assumed she'd left with Ariel.

"Mrs. Bane, are you all right? What are you doing here? Is there anyone else in the back?" He nods toward the restrooms and back hallway. Candy's wild eyes move in and out of focus. She struggles with the nasal cannula. She points to the oxygen tank connected to the back of her chair.

Jack runs to her and checks the levels. It's on red. "Mrs. Bane, let's get you out of here. Your oxygen is empty. The firefighters will be here any minute. I think Connie may be with them—he mentioned he had to work late tonight, covering a shift."

Jack grips the back of Candy's chair and begins to push her toward the front entrance of the atrium.

73

nside the burning storeroom, Hannah passes out.

"Sam!" Sara calls as Hannah's head lolls to one side.

"Hannah! Wake up!" Sam wails as he pulls with all his strength on the plastic zip ties. Every muscle in his body burns with effort, but the plastic only gets tighter and tighter. It cuts into his skin. Sara nudges Hannah with her head, trying to rouse her, but she's not breathing.

Alarmed and panicked, Sam pushes himself upward, but can't find his balance to stand. He is suddenly dizzy and green. Before he can try again to get to Hannah, he leans over and vomits on the floor.

In the corner, Sara's jeans catch a flame, and she expels a startled gasp. Sara slams her legs against the walls to try to snuff it out. Next second, the entire shelving system in the storeroom, superheated and melting, creaks and begins to fall. It's heavy weight plummets toward Hannah and Sara.

The burning mass falls like cut timber, unstoppable. Sara covers Hannah's head with her zip-tied arms and as much of her body as she can.

Sam holds his head and wails in pain. Between his fingers, his brown hair turns silver in his hands, which morph into an older man's rough and stubby fingers. When Sam raises his head, Sara gasps at what she sees—a large, gray-haired man bursting the buttons on Sam's suit shirt. His chest heaves, and his eyes turn from dark brown to bright green.

With only a millisecond to spare, Conrad Bane Sr. leaps through the air and catches the falling shelves in his massive hands, still zip tied. The force knocks him to the ground, but he lands just shy of Sara and Hannah, jumbled in a mess of smoking metal, burnt supplies, and boxes.

Before anyone can move, Hannah's eyes flutter open. Involuntarily, she screams from behind her gag, her face trained on the giant gray-haired man that used be Sam.

Sara wants to call out—to scream—but her throat is locked and filled with rising smoke. She chokes. Conrad Sr. scans the debris and wedges one edge of his zip tie around a sharp metal point from the broken shelving unit. The ties split, and his hands are free. He finds a box cutter on the floor and cuts off Sara's and Hannah's restraints. Hannah clutches the garbage bag and pulls it down away from her mouth. She tries to breathe but chokes on the thick gray smoke.

Without hesitation, Conrad Sr. collects Hannah in his massive arms and pushes open the emergency door to the alley with his foot. He carries the teenager outside and deposits her in the alleyway. Sara follows and both suck in fresh air, gasping wildly. Their eyes water as they take in life-giving oxygen.

A minute later, still oblivious to the emergency, Travis looks up from the loading dock wall at the commotion. His eyes widen as Hannah, covered in soot and smoke, runs to him.

74

In the atrium, the fire creeps up the cavernous room. Outside the entrance, two fire trucks, three ambulances, and a dozen firefighters connect hoses and swarm toward the building. The atrium's sprinkler system is fully operational now, and water blankets the empty stage, unoccupied tables, and deserted bar area.

Jack rolls Candy past a fiery potted palm tree near the bar area, and the sleeve of her shirt catches a flame. Quickly, she pats it out with her free hand, empty of the pistol, now hidden in her saddlebag. Candy scans the scene for her son but doesn't see him. A firefighter runs toward her.

"Over here!" Jack calls.

Before the firefighter can reach them, an ear-shattering blast emanates from the high, glass ceiling. On the side of the atrium near the bird hospital, where the fire burns unabated, flames connect with the decorative wooden structures bolted high in the air above the netting. The hawk, falcon, and owl on display for the party screech loudly in alarm. They fly in circles above their flaming perches. As Jack and Candy follow the birds with upturned gazes, a large pane of glass, overheated by the flames, cracks into two large shards.

Before their eyes, the giant crystal sheets slice through the netting and rocket toward them. Before either can respond to the threat, Conrad Bane Sr. envelops Candy with one massive arm and grabs Jack with the other, covering them, now a tangled bunch on the wheelchair, with his body. Blades of glass bounce off his broad back like popcorn.

Candy cowers under the weight of the stranger.

For a moment, time stops. Conrad Bane Sr. pulls back so Candy and Jack can see him. The woman's eyes take a few seconds to adjust. Jack does a double take. In unison they call out, "Conrad!" and "Mr. Bane?"

Candy reaches for her husband. "Oh my God! It's my Conrad! He's come back to me!" Conrad Bane Sr. gazes at Candy with a mix of pity and warmth.

A second later, a shard of glass the size of a butcher knife falls from the ceiling and stabs Jack mercilessly in the leg. He bellows in pain, and his leg spurts blood.

In one quick movement, Conrad jumps over Candy in the chair and reaches Jack. The hulking man hastily removes the glass from Jack's leg, pulls Sam's leather belt from around his own waist, and cinches Jack's bleeding leg like a vice.

Above their heads, a loud screech sounds as the falcon, hawk, and owl soar out of the opening caused by the shattering of the glass. The birds fly away into the dark, clear night.

The firefighter, momentarily stunned by what just occurred, springs into action and grabs the handles on Candy's wheelchair. He spins her toward to the exit. Behind him, medics rush toward Jack, who is bleary-eyed with pain.

"No!" Candy wails as the firefighter wheels her away. She reaches for Conrad Sr., now slumped on the floor, a heap of tattered clothing.

"Conrad!" Candy yells. She twists and struggles in the chair to see her husband again, but the moment has passed. In his place, Sam sits up and holds his head in pain.

Candy howls, "Nooooo! Don't leave me again, Conrad! Don't leave. . . ." She bows her head and slumps into a sobbing mess. The firefighter rolls her past emergency personnel toward the entrance of the atrium.

In a crazy instant, Candy reaches into the saddlebag attached to her wheelchair. She retrieves the pistol and, with an unexpected burst of energy, jumps from the chair. She sidesteps the firefighter and points the gun at Sam, now getting to his feet.

"You bring my Conrad back!" she wails at Sam.

The firefighter escorting Candy to safety is stunned by the old woman's actions. For a moment, he freezes in confusion.

Sam puts up his hands. "Candy, be calm. That's not how it works. I can't bring him back. You don't need to do this. Just put down the gun."

Jack yells from the floor, where paramedics load him onto a gurney, "Candy, no!"

Other first responders run towards Candy as her escort finally reacts, reaching for the gun. Before any of the shocked witnesses can make a move, Candy fires.

Sam cringes in anticipation of the bullet, but there is none. Candy's knees buckle, and she drops to the floor. Blood soaks her shirt. She looks at her bleeding stomach in shock before she slumps to the floor, dropping the gun.

Sam, Jack, the paramedics, and the firefighters all look up to see Conrad Bane Jr. at the front door of the atrium, gun drawn. He slowly lowers it and hands it back to Jimmy, who eyes his empty holster in surprise.

Conrad calls out weakly, "Ma." He runs to his mother.

75

Red-and-blue lights fill the smoke-filled atrium, reflecting off the shattered glass and remaining ceiling tiles. Detective Kelly, Jimmy, a bald officer, and two EMTs enter the smoking remains of the atrium. The fire is now out completely, but the burnt shell of the bird hospital and storeroom still smoke.

Conrad rocks his mother, holding her on his lap. "I'm sorry, Ma. I couldn't let you hurt anyone else." Conrad looks at Sam. "I'm sorry, Sam. I'm so sorry. I didn't know until the detectives told me about Paulo tonight. I found plans, devices, and Dad's old uniform in her room about two weeks ago." His eyes water. "I told her to get rid of all of it because I thought she was holding on too tight. To memories, or whatever. But I didn't realize what she was planning to do. I didn't know about the fires. Or her plan to set up Paulo."

He fights emotion but loses control. Conrad holds his mother. "How could you, Ma? We're having a baby. Your grandbaby. How could you hurt all those people?"

Sam doesn't say a word. He watches as Candy's lifeless body is removed from her son's arms and loaded onto a gurney. Jimmy escorts Conrad outside.

Detective Kelly and Sam head outside. "Jack's with his wife at the hospital. They're stitching up his leg, but he'll be okay. Ariel Bane is undergoing an emergency C-section. We'd just finished questioning Conrad at the fire station when they got the call"—the detective indicates the atrium with a wave of the hand—"about the fire here. Conrad's family was at this event, including Candy, so we came straight away. Conrad had just come clean about what he'd found in Candy's room a couple of weeks ago. Same stuff we found in Paulo's garage."

Sam and Detective Kelly both watch Connie being escorted into a police van outside the atrium.

"Do you believe him? That he had nothing to do with it?" Sam asks.

Detective Kelly shrugs. "Don't know. Maybe he knows more than we think. His shock over what happened to Paulo seemed real enough. Who knows? Maybe he would have done anything to save his mother . . . or maybe having a baby put things in perspective for him."

The two men approach an ambulance. Hannah runs to her uncle, and they embrace for a long, silent moment. Sara joins them, followed by a bewildered Travis.

Sam looks up as Detective Kelly heads toward the police van. "Maybe Conrad did what he felt needed to be done for the sake of his family. In the end."

"Maybe so," says Detective Kelly. He puts up a hand in goodbye. "Maybe so."

76

Sam, Sara, and Hannah sit together at a metal table in the open-air patio of a boutique downtown hotel. The evening air is mild, and only a few passersby stroll down the avenue past the threesome; with the exception of the white-aproned young waitress periodically refilling their sweet teas, the group is alone.

They are fine with the silence. The waitress clears dinner plates, confirms no one is in the mood for cheesecake, and retreats inside. Hannah gazes at the remains of the atrium a few blocks in the distance. She sees yellow tape and a few security guards buzzing around the perimeter, but emergency personnel are gone, having wrapped up their investigation two days prior.

Hannah gazes at her uncle. His stubble has popped out into the beginnings of a beard, and his skin is sallow. He is exhausted, as they all are. Hannah's eyes then shift to Sara, who looks equally worn, with glasses atop her slightly oily brown ponytail. Sara lays a hand on Sam's arm, gently. Sam sighs deeply at Sara, and then at Hannah.

Hannah hopes they can all remain there, sans dialogue, for a while longer. There is nothing else to say or sign or discuss. It tires her, trying to constantly overenunciate words she can only hear as a muffled drone, even with her hearing aid in place. Her uncle is a pretty good signer, but he's slow at times and has to think about words and phrases, many times bungling them in funny ways.

With Travis it's different. Sign language, body language, and the language of the eyes all come naturally to him. And to many of their friends at school. They all grew up with no or limited hearing, and it's how they all interpret the world already—gestures, interpretations of the smallest nuances of human movement. It really is amazing; Hannah often thinks how much communication between people is intuitive and based in physical—and maybe mental or spiritual—signals rather than words.

Hannah didn't understand everything that had happened the night of the fire, and she didn't really care that much. She was just happy it was over, and they were home again. Sam had tried to explain the big gray-haired man, but then gave up. He'd said it was like writing the letters only more intense. That instead of just his hand, his entire body was being directed.

Ending up at the bird place was really weird to Hannah. She had remembered visiting the bird rescue with her mom a few years ago. The center actually had an injured eagle that had arrived for specialized surgery on one of its talons. Really rare, they said. The Raptor Institute, the guide had told them, cared for a lot of owls, hawks, and even falcons, but hardly ever an eagle.

Hannah was shorter then, maybe twelve, but on tiptoes could see the recuperating bird through the glass walls of the hospital area. The bird had sat up and trained amazing dark eyes directly on Hannah. Hannah waved at the animal, and she swore the eagle blinked its eyes and opened its beak right back at her. It was the only movement the bird could make, since its wings and legs were secured as it recovered.

Her mom had gone on and on about that bird. They had grabbed a hot dog after leaving the atrium at one of the stands that serviced all the bankers and young professionals scooting around Center City in suits and heels.

"Wasn't that amazing?" her mom had marveled, mouth crammed full of ketchup and bun.

Hannah couldn't understand, of course, and shook her head.

Her mom had chuckled, stuck the hot dog under one arm, and flapped her "wings" dramatically for effect. Hannah laughed at the sight. Her mom was always so silly.

Hannah's attention is brought back to the table as Sam's phone vibrates. He speaks to someone for a few minutes, and Sara excuses herself to the ladies' room.

Hannah thinks of the eagle paintings. She knows that the image—repeating over and over again for the last few months—was from her mom. It must have been the only way her mom knew how to reach out from wherever she was now.

The heavy feeling in her chest threatens to overcome her again, and so she breathes in deeply and thinks about Travis instead. They have to see each other soon. She misses him.

Sam hangs up the phone. "Detective Kelly"—he nods at the phone and sticks it back in his pocket—"needs to see me tomorrow. Something about the judge's letter."

Hannah gestures quickly to him, and he nods.

"Yes," Sam says. "The letter you mailed. That I told you not to. To that judge, remember? Got me into a lot o' hot water." Sam smiles a little behind the chastisement.

Hannah reddens a little and signs, "Sorry . . . not sorry," and smiles widely.

77

Jimmy escorts Sam through backhoes, shovels, and police tape. Mounds of dirt and broken concrete line the fence.

"Turns out when the judge's wife saw your letter, the message from Cecilia"—Jimmy shrugs, a little embarrassed at the entire idea of Sam channeling messages—"or whatever it was, she thought it was time to tell us about her husband's odd behavior around the time of their daughter's disappearance. Putting in a pool in the middle of winter, for example."

Jimmy directs Sam around the brick house, past crime-scene investigators, to an expansive backyard. The elaborate pool area, outdoor living space, and stone patio are turned upside down—debris, stone, and piles of dirt litter the yard. Jimmy sighs and points to a cluster of masked-and-gloved investigators bent over a mound of broken pool tile. "We found Cecilia Mason's body this morning." Jimmy shook his head. "She was only eight years old, for Christ's sake."

Sam closes his eyes and breathes.

"We would've never found her, if it wasn't for you, Sam," Jimmy says gravely.

"I didn't . . . I don't want to be part of this," Sam replies. "It makes me sick."

"I know. But take solace in the fact that Cecilia's voice was heard. By you. You made that possible for her. You gave her soul some peace."

Jimmy leads Sam back out onto the street.

At his car door, Jimmy says, "You're free to go, Sam. The arson investigation is ongoing, but the fire marshal thinks we have enough physical evidence to tie all the fires back to Candy Bane."

Sam nods in sad agreement and shakes Jimmy's hand. "Thanks for everything, Jimmy. For believing me. At least a little."

Jimmy smiles. "You'd make a fair cop, you know."

Sam shakes his head. "Thanks, but I don't have the stomach for it."

78

Sam, Sara, and Hannah sit on one side of a patio table overlooking Lake Norman. Jack, Kate, and Indy chow down on burgers and fries across from them. Behind them, light bounces off blue water, and a pontoon boat travels lazily toward the horizon. Soft rock music, emanating from the bar area, plays in the background.

Jack wipes mustard from his mouth and swallows a gulp of beer. "Uh, I'm gonna need a judge's ruling on that. Alex and Conrad Sr. were cosmically tied together on the other side?"

Sara sips iced tea and nods. "It actually makes sense," she says. "The spirits of Conrad Sr. and Alex were linked when she died by Candy's hand while covering the Azhartec fire."

Indy raises neon-blue sunglasses and blinks in the sun. He rocks back in his chair and rubs his belly. "Well, it's only a theory, but we believe that Conrad Sr. and the spirits that were connected to him may have used Alex's connection to Sam to accomplish their own ends. To finish unfinished business, so to speak."

Hannah taps Sam on the shoulder, and they sign to each other. Hannah nods in understanding.

Kate sips a margarita. "I cannot wait to tell my book club about this. It's all so interesting." She turns to Sara. "After Hannah's prom, when you told me about the way Sam's letter saved that woman, Carol Graham . . . I mean, how terrifying—the guy in the closet and all that? O-M-G, really. But Sam's letter saved her! My book club was so—"

Jack smiles at his wife. "Is there a point to this story, honey, or should I order another beer?"

Kate slaps him playfully on the shoulder. "Okay, whatever, but I was shocked by all this." She turns to Sam. "We've known you for so long, Sam. You are, like, the most practical person I know. I just can't believe all this."

Sam nods. "Neither can I, Kate."

Sara asks, "What about your book club?"

"Oh," Kate says, getting back on point. "After I heard about the story with Sam writing that letter from Alice, Carol's grandmother, that saved her life and all, we started reading, like, really deep and spiritual books. You know, instead of *Fifty Shades*."

"Oh?" Sara says. "Like what?"

"*Eat, Pray, Love*," Kate answers.

Jack pats his belly and holds out a hand. "I *eat* so much I *pray* for an antacid, my *love*."

Sam and Indy boo mildly at the terrible joke.

"What?" Jack says, ducking a napkin from Kate.

Hannah smiles and gazes at the lake, losing interest in the adult conversation.

"Seriously, Jack," Sara continues. "Remember the treasure you and Sam found with that young couple from Statesville?"

Jack nods. "Yeah, that was really weird. The stuff that Sam wrote out on the bathroom paper towel led them to dig up the old Civil War chest. I was ten seconds away from calling the loony bin and chucking Sam straight inside."

Sam chuckles. "Thanks, partner."

Jack shrugs. "Well . . ."

Sara pushes a stray lock of brown hair behind one ear. "I had my grad students do some research on the old letters in the treasure chest found on the Jacksons' property. It turns out that Conrad Sr.'s great-great grandfather, Earl Bane, was likely the Union solider that visited Beulah that day. Earl brought that treasure to Melvin's family to pay them back for Melvin's act of charity—for saving Earl's life on the battlefield."

Jack finishes his beer in one gulp and raises an eyebrow skeptically.

Sam nods. "It's true, Jack. I also found out from Detective Kelly that Judge Mason was the Banes' neighbor in New York, years ago. Another connection."

"Little Cecilia's spirit wrote that letter to her father, and justice was done," Sara says.

Indy slurps on a chocolate milk shake. "Yeah, and the special recipe for cornbread was sent to Michelle Britt." Indy tips his chair forward, and it lands on all fours. "Britt is the maiden name of Michelle Bane, Conrad Jr.'s sister-in-law." Indy slaps a hand across his forehead. "Ouch. Brain freeze."

"What about Carol Graham? The woman saved by the letter from her grandmother, Alice?" Kate says, leaning on one hand.

"Alice Graham was a flight attendant," Sam says. "She trained in New York City for a summer before she was married."

"And guess who her fire-rescue trainer was?" Sara asks.

Jack shakes his head. "No way. Conrad Sr.?"

Sara and Sam nod.

Jack humps the table indiscreetly. "Did they ever—?"

Sara nods.

Hannah, catching Jack's mime, says, "Gross."

"Yep," Sara continues. "We found a former pilot here in Charlotte that worked with her. He and some other crew knew about Alice's affair with the tall, handsome firefighter from New York."

Jack yells, "Get out!" He pauses. "And the message on the board about Paulo? Or the shaving cream Sam told us about?"

"I would say those were from Alex directly to Sam." Indy nods enthusiastically.

Sara takes a sip of sweet tea. "I wonder if Paulo had been home after you received that message at Hannah's school, if that would have made a difference."

Sam smiles sadly. "It's possible. He may have mentioned the supplies in the garage . . . Candy's irrationally cruel behavior towards him. Maybe something would have tipped us off."

Jack shrugs and sighs deeply.

"In the end, we believe that all these connections were possible because of the incredible bond between Sam and Alex."

Everyone at the table looks at Sam. He stares at his plate. His eyes sting, and he looks into the distance at the water.

Kate, oblivious to Sam's discomfort, asks, "Sam, have you had any other episodes? Letters or messages or whatever?"

Sam shakes his head. "No. Nothing."

Indy jumps in. "When Sam solved the arson cases, we think he broke the connection. Between him and Alex."

Sam stands. "Bathroom." He heads inside.

Jack watches his partner for a second and decides to leave him alone. He turns back to the table. "Well, you guys are the experts. Although you pinned Connie wrong."

Sara shakes her head. "That's my fault. Conrad's handwriting was almost identical to his mother's. I missed the slant in the lowercase *n*."

"Yeah, that happens to me all the time," Jack says.

Sara smiles.

Jack checks out the inside bar and doesn't see Sam returning yet. He speaks quietly. "But what happened to Sam in the atrium? I swore I saw Connie's dad, like, for real."

Sara and Hannah exchange looks. Hannah signs while saying, "So did we."

Sara nods. "We can only assume that Conrad Sr. finally used the connection himself—to save us and Candy from the fire. To make things right."

"Maybe it was his way of making something up to Sam," Indy muses.

Sara smiles to herself. "Maybe Alex made him do it. I wouldn't put it past her." She looks up to see Sam returning.

Indy stands and stretches. "Well, amigos, I think it's time for me to jam." He turns to Jack. "Catch my lecture on physical manifestation of spirit bodies next week. I'll put your name on the audit list." Indy smiles.

"Sure, I'll do that," Jack says with a wink.

Dr. Indy jumps up and pops the wheels on his sneaker-skates.

"Big date?" Sam says, laying cash down on the check and covering it with a saltshaker.

"Nah," Indy says, rolling away. "Just some research."

Sam calls after him. "With Molly?"

Indy raises a hand without looking back and skates out of sight.

79

On a bustling city street flanked by a mix of high-rise bank buildings, outdoor cafés, and parking garages, Sam watches Hannah through a shop window. She inspects a new set of paints and brushes.

A female voice startles him from the sidewalk behind. "Well, look who it is, Lincoln."

Sam turns to see Madame Amanda waddling toward him with a baby strapped to her chest. Lincoln is in tow, sucking on a lollipop.

Sam waves hello.

Lincoln giggles wildly.

Amanda nods to the next-door beauty shop, Amanda's Cut & Color. "Just checking up on the girls, making sure they're not burnin' the joint down."

Sam peers inside the high-end shop. "Wow. *This* is your beauty shop?"

Madame Amanda nods at a tall, svelte woman with a freshly cut bob as she exits her shop and passes by. "We do all right downtown. It's amazin' how much these city gals pay for a cut and color if you do it with a glass o' wine on the side."

Sam smiles.

Amanda nods toward Hannah through the art-store window as she approaches the checkout line inside. "That's gotta be Hannah. Looks just like her mama."

Sam smiles warmly at his niece, then turns to Amanda. "Listen, I wanted to thank you."

Amanda pats the sleeping baby's back and yanks on Lincoln's arm as he reaches for a wad of gum on the ground. "Uh-uh, Lincoln. Leave it." She turns to Sam. "For what? I didn't think you took too kindly to my eye gazing."

Sam smiles. "I wanted to thank you for being a friend to Alex. I know she must have appreciated it."

Amanda smiles. "It was me who was lucky. She was a bright spirit in this dull world."

"She was."

The baby on Amanda's chest coos softly. "Haven't heard from her lately?"

Sam shakes his head. "No."

Hannah exits the art shop into bright sunshine. She smiles and coos at the baby, who squeals in a joyful stretch.

Lincoln tugs on his mother's skirt.

"All right, Lincoln, we're goin'." Amanda looks at Sam and Hannah. "We have a date with a dinosaur." She nods toward the natural history museum, which sports a gigantic poster of dino skeletons on its front.

"Bye, Amanda. Bye, Lincoln," Sam says, turning to leave. As the two parties nod goodbye, Sam turns back. "What's her name?" He nods to the bundle. "The baby?"

Madame Amanda looks lovingly at the baby girl on her chest. "Alexandra," she says proudly. "But I call her Alex."

80

Alex

My days at the construction zone are about to be over. Big Gray was a stand-up guy. He's gone now, and I'm the only one left here. It's quiet—just what I always wanted. Maybe too quiet. But I believe I'm destined for other things soon. There's a sense of peace here now. I can't really sort out all the details. It's more of a feeling that the story—at least this bit of it—has been completed. My part of Sam and Hannah's story is done, but I think it will live on as they do. I am feeling free now, and I wonder where it all will lead.

There is one more thing I want to do before I go, though. And then I'll leave you with this. I have come to understand that no story really ever ends. It just keeps floating and transforming and flying overhead, far above us, looking down with nothing but love.

81

Sam walks through a vast, gently sloping cemetery. He passes through an old section laden with crumbling, unreadable markers that appear to be dated around the mid-eighteenth century. In the newer section, the trees are sparse and provide less protection for the permanent residents. Elaborate marble stones and aboveground tombs bear the names of prominent local families alongside flat stones that mark simple, unadorned resting places.

Sam stands over a fresh grave mounded with dirt and marked only with a laminated paper sign and a simple inscription: *Paulo Vargas (1995–2019)*. Piled all around the weathered temporary marker are flowers, stuffed animals, photos, and other memorabilia. Sam thinks about the service held for this young man and the terrible loss felt by his cousin, Ariel.

Ariel had told Sam and Jack after the service that Paulo was a good man, an honest man. The only reason he lied about how Consuela was killed—by terrorists and not a bus accident—was that he didn't want her memory to be tainted forever with their mark. He didn't want them to win. He

238

wanted to remember her as she'd been—a beautiful and brilliant researcher who loved her birds and dedicated her life to their preservation.

Sam takes a moment in silence to bless Paulo and Consuela and all who have lost, even himself. He bends and adds a small silver eagle charm to the other signs of affection. "Rest in peace, Paulo."

❧

Sam sits next to his sister's grave, cross-legged. The dirt that covers it has leveled off some, and her stone is in place. A simple upright granite marker bears her name, the dates of her life, and the words Beloved Daughter, Sister, Mother, and Friend.

Sam picks tufts of grass and flicks them away. The day is pleasant, and birds chirp lightly in a nearby oak tree. "I haven't had any more . . . problems, so that's good. Maybe it's done now that it's . . . that we know now . . . that it's resolved."

Sam surveys the oak. It's at least a hundred years old. The roots have tumbled the earth below it like the dark tentacles of a monster, and the branches reach so high he can't see the sky through its canopy.

"Hannah is doing great. She's a young lady now. You should see her . . ."

He sits in silence a moment and allows himself some tears. "I miss you, Alex."

Sam breathes deeply. Although he's alone, he is self-conscious of his tears and dries them with a tissue from his pocket.

"I just wish you had talked to me about something personal. About us." Sam hits the ground hard with a fist. "All that time, I just wanted to hear your voice again. Through all this crap, this ridiculous shit, the only person I really ever wanted to hear from was you."

All is silent save for the breeze and the birds.

Sam takes a last look at Alex's gravestone and moves to push himself up. Before he can make it to standing, his stomach roils with nausea, but the feeling passes quickly. Within a second, his hand moves on its own again. It picks up a stick and scrawls in the dirt.

He stares at the ground in front of him, reading the message.

I love you, Sammy.

Sam is stunned. "Alex? Is that you? Or like, just a weird projection of my subconscious? Or what would Dr. Patel say—that I want it all too much, that it doesn't work that way?" Sam claps himself over the mouth to stop his babbling. He says to no one in particular, "Sorry."

The next moment, a squeal breaks the breezy silence of the cemetery. Sam looks up from the grass at the old oak tree a few yards away. He hadn't noticed this before, but there is an old wooden swing hanging from a high branch.

Alex's spirit swings gleefully on the plank. She looks like a photo in Sam's study—one taken at Sam's high school graduation—where brother and sister were young and full of life. Sam's eyes widen. He blinks and stares wordlessly. At long last, he sees his sister, and she's flying free, as she always did.

Before his eyes, a shadow appears at the top of the tall oak tree. Sam doesn't want to take his eyes from Alex, but a loud screech forces his eyes up. A large bald eagle lands on the tree's crown with a rustle, shaking out its wings in a magnificent spread.

Somewhere in his memory, Sam recalls a story about the bald eagle making a comeback around North Carolina lakes. But . . . this was . . . was this real? Laughing in awe, eyes on the eagle, Sam yells to his sister, "Look up, Alex. It's an eagle!"

When Sam looks back down to his sister, the swing is empty. It moves gently back and forth. Sam stares at it for a moment. And then it, too, is gone. The silence is broken by the call of the eagle, who takes off in broad-winged flight.

Sam swallows hard. "I love you too, Alex."

Sam sits and watches the tree for a long while. As dusk begins to settle and shadows start to surface, Sam finally stands and leaves the cemetery.

As Sam walks away, he is watched over from high in the darkening sky by the soaring bird. The eagle calls to him through the darkness. Freedom is its cry.

THE END

ABOUT THE AUTHOR

T.E. Lane enjoys writing commercial fiction with a mystical twist. Hailing from the Southeast United States, the author enjoys weaving in locales, characters, and situations that feel familiar with just a touch of magic or otherworldly influence. A fan of action, thriller, mystery, and literary fiction, the author enjoys blending aspects of many genres into a single work, creating a unique experience that will keep readers turning the pages. From the shores of south Florida to the mountains of the Carolinas, T.E. Lane creates worlds you'll want to inhabit with characters that make you feel right at home.

IngramElliott Publishing

IngramElliott is an award-winning independent publisher with a mission to bring great stories to light in print and on-screen. We publish stories that will translate well into film, broadcast, and streaming television projects across many popular genres. We look for a great story, unique voice, and the author's ability to build a strong platform. Please review our current submission guidelines for more information.

IE Snaps! by IngramElliott

Our IE Snaps! imprint features novella-length genre fiction in favorite genres like action, thriller, mystery, romance, and young adult. These titles are designed for a quick read on the go. Visit our website for all of our IngramElliott and IE Snaps! titles and to follow us on social media.

www.ingramelliott.com